Tempting the Duchess

Disgraceful Duchesses, Book 2

Sara Bennett

DRAGONBLADE PUBLISHING, INC.

Dragonblade Publishing, Inc. is an imprint of Kathryn Le Veque Novels, Inc.
P.O. Box 23
Moreno Valley, CA 92556
ceo@dragonbladepublishing.com

Produced in the United States of America

First Edition August 2024
Trade Paperback Edition

ARE YOU SIGNED UP FOR DRAGONBLADE'S BLOG?

You'll get the latest news and information on exclusive giveaways, exclusive excerpts, coming releases, sales, free books, cover reveals and more.

Check out our complete list of authors, too!

No spam, no junk. That's a promise!

Sign Up Here

www.dragonbladepublishing.com

Dearest Reader;

Thank you for your support of a small press. At Dragonblade Publishing, we strive to bring you the highest quality Historical Romance from some of the best authors in the business. Without your support, there is no 'us', so we sincerely hope you adore these stories and find some new favorite authors along the way.

Happy Reading!

CEO, Dragonblade Publishing

Chapter One

T HE ROAD THROUGH the forest was rough and far too narrow for the ducal coach, but they had had no choice but to take it. Ellis heard the shouts and knew her pursuers were close behind. She could not afford to be caught. She had known when she set out that this was her one chance, and if it failed . . . well, *that* was just too awful to contemplate.

The vehicle lurched, tipped to one side, and began to fall. The sound of raised voices and whinnying horses spun around her as her world turned upside down. Then, silence. She lay sprawled over the plush seat, shaken and dazed. She had bumped her head as the coach went over, and now it began to ache. No time to feel sorry for herself. The door was wrenched open and Ellis shrank back, eyes wide, fearing the worst.

But it was Rowan, her groom, peering down at her. He had a bloody cut on his craggy cheek and his eyes were wild.

"My lady," he said urgently, "you must get out. Hide in the forest. It is your only chance."

As if to underline his words, a pistol shot echoed through the trees.

Scrambling up, Ellis reached for his outstretched hand. In an instant she was pulled up through the open door. Anxiously she thought of her bag, the few things she had been able to pack before she fled, but there was no time. Rowan gave her a push toward the dense trees—"Run!"—and a moment later she was running, her black skirts tangling about her legs and the soles of her feet in her thin slippers already bruised from the rough ground. She should have worn more sensible outdoor clothing, but she had thought she would be more likely to convince Theo that her call upon her neighbor was genuine if she wore her "visiting" dress and slippers.

And he had seemed convinced.

She had thought she was safely away from him.

Now she wondered if he had known all along and only fooled her into believing she was safe. What better way to dispose of her than to blame highwaymen and leave himself the innocent? Sir Theo Abergele wanted the house and estate, he wanted everything that had become hers after her husband—and Theo's cousin—the Duke of Breamore, had died. The estate was not entailed, and it had been solely up to Archie to decide who would inherit. Although it was unusual to choose his wife as his heir, Archie had decided upon Ellis, much to Theo's fury. And when she had rejected his subsequent offer of marriage, Ellis had known the chance for her escape was narrowing.

You have no right to all of this! She could still hear Theo's savage words as he stood glaring at her in the formal drawing room. Before now the business of burying Archie had taken precedence over all else. It was a quiet funeral—the duke had led a quiet life on his estate on the Welsh border—but he was genuinely mourned. There was still so much to do, but Theo could not wait. Her heart had sunk when she saw the pitiless gleam in his eyes, and she had known that the conversation she had been sidestepping since Archie took ill could no longer be avoided.

I know your marriage was not consummated. How could it be? It was all a sham.

Prove it! she had hissed back at him. *Your cousin was well-loved. No one here will speak against him.*

His eyes, so like Archie's and yet so different, had turned to ice. *Then you have two choices. Marry me.*

Never! What is the other choice? Her heart had been beating wildly.

He hadn't answered, had instead shown his teeth in a savage smile. And if she had been afraid of him before, now she was terrified.

Thank God her servants were loyal. Theo would not get anything from them, no matter what threats he issued, although she did not want to imagine what their loyalty would cost them. While she had wanted to stand up for them and protect them, the truth was she couldn't even protect herself.

There was another pistol shot, this one from behind her, in the direction of the abandoned coach. She said a swift prayer for Rowan's safety. Theo would want no witnesses to his evil deed, and she prayed the groom had taken his own advice and vanished into the forest, too. Rowan knew the countryside well. Surely, he would be all right.

It was gloomy in the forest, the sunlight barely penetrating through the stands of Welsh oaks. Ellis had never been comfortable in places like this—there was something ominous about them. She felt as if she was being watched by the ancient peoples who had once inhabited them. She just hoped there was a way out.

But no matter how she looked about her, there was nothing. All she could do was continue to push through the undergrowth and trust to chance.

A prickly shrub caught her skirt, jerking her backward with a startled cry and tearing the black cloth of her mourning dress, reminding her why she wore it. Archie, her husband was dead. Tears threatened, but she held them back. There would be time enough to grieve when she was safe. Archie would not want her to fall into his cousin's clutches. He had believed he had many more years to live, but the fever had taken him off so swiftly, there had barely been time for last goodbyes.

Her sorrowful thoughts accompanied her as she wandered, seemingly endlessly. Everything looked the same, and for all she knew she could be walking in circles. She wasn't sure how long it had been since the coach overturned, and then in the hush of the woodland Ellis heard voices. They were faint and growing fainter, but she was not fooled into thinking they were friendly. Her only hope was to outrun and outwit Theo and his henchmen.

And then what? Reside among the trees like some wild creature, drinking from puddles and eating berries and sleeping on a high branch? The thought of the Duchess of Breamore living such a life brought hysterical laughter bubbling to her lips. She had become so used to the luxury of being Archie's wife, her every wish granted—within reason of course—that she had begun to believe she had always lived that way. It wasn't true. She had been brought up to a simple life and a happy one. All that had changed when her father died in a riding accident, and putting food on their table became a daily chore. That was before her mother took Ellis and her two sisters to London in a desperate throw of the dice.

You cannot be so beautiful without a reason!

It had worked. They had taken the *ton* by storm and were much sought after. Ellis could have had her pick of many eligible men, but the attention had gone to her mother's head, and she had declared her daughters must be duchesses. To the amazement of London society, all three *had* married dukes. But as for happiness . . .? Ellis had believed she was probably the happiest of the three. The lucky one.

Until Archie died.

How long had she been wandering around? Hours. She had started out on her visit not long after lunch, which now seemed a lifetime ago. Ahead of her the gloomy forest seemed to lighten. Hardly allowing herself to believe it, she took one step, and then another. The trees had thinned, and now they were younger and less imposing. She had reached the very edge of the forest and now stood in the warm, golden summer evening. There, before her, was a sweep of green fields dotted with grazing sheep.

As peaceful as the pastoral scene was, it did not hold her

attention for long. Because beyond the fields and the sheep, rising out of a lush garden, was a house.

It was a two-story dwelling made of soft grey stone that seemed to glow in the evening light. Mullioned windows dotted the frontage—or was it the side of the house she was looking at?—and smoke drifted from its chimneys.

Ellis caught her breath. If there was smoke, then there must be someone inside. Would they help her? Excitement fizzled into doubt. How did she know the people who lived there were not friends of Theo's?

And yet she had no choice but to risk it. She could not hide here for much longer. Soon it would be dark, and she could not stay in the forest or wander the countryside—Theo would surely find her. The house was her best chance of safety.

There was a low stone wall to mark the separation of the fields from the forest, and it was only as Ellis began to climb over it that she realized she had lost one of her slippers. As she dropped to the other side, she looked down at herself with a grimace. As well as a rend in her gown, there were tears in her stockings, and her hair had lost its pins and was tumbling down over her shoulders in a tangled mess. Impatiently she pushed back the dark locks and flinched as she became aware of the stinging scratches on her hands.

During her flight she had been too focused on staying out of Theo's clutches to notice her injuries, but now her body ached and itched and stung.

She must look like a mad woman. Would the occupants of the house slam the door in her face? Anxiously she glanced behind her at the forest, but if there was anyone watching her from its murky depths, then they were well hidden.

Ellis limped onward in her one slipper, making her way diagonally across the field toward what appeared to be a drive running between the sheep pastures. It *was* a drive. She stood and looked down its length at the house. A gatehouse framed the front entrance, while the building's solid structure made her suspect it had started life as a fortified manor. Somewhere the inhabitants could shelter in times of unrest. And there had been a great deal of unrest on the Welsh borders over the centuries.

Her home, Breamore, must be miles away. She had already travelled some distance before she'd reached the forest, and who knew how far she had run after that? She was certain she had never visited the house standing before her. For good reason, Archie's household had been an insular one, and Ellis was acquainted with only one or two of their neighbors, in particular Mrs. Garrett, the woman she had told Theo she was going to visit after lunch today.

She set off again. Two stone lions guarded the front door, their expressions grim enough to frighten away strangers. Ellis noticed a walled garden to her left, the plants lush and inviting, but her focus was on the solid-looking door. It had a brass knocker that was fashioned into another lion.

She lifted it and let it fall. The noise it made didn't seem loud enough to attract much attention, so she did it again. Twice.

"Please," she whispered, and shot a frantic glance behind her. The sheep were still grazing, and the forest was still silently watching. At any moment Theo could burst from the trees and come riding toward her. She would fight him with everything she had, but she knew she would not win.

You will be safe, Archie had whispered to her as he lay dying. *I have left everything to you. My man of business will see that you are cared for.*

But his man of business had been turned by Theo's inducements, and Ellis was anything but safe. With Archie gone and the servants afraid, there had only been Rowan brave enough to help her leave, and now there was no one.

The screech of a peacock startled a cry from her. The creature was strutting along the garden wall, as if showing off its gloriously colored plumage. Ellis's heart seemed about to jump from her chest, and her knees shook as if she might collapse. She leaned against the door to hold herself upright. There was still no sound from inside, so she pounded on the wood with her fist, once, twice, and was about to do it a third time, when finally the door was opened.

"Are you trying to wake the dead?" growled a man's voice.

With her support taken abruptly away from her, Ellis staggered and would have fallen if a strong hand had not closed around her arm and held her upright. Breathless, anxious, she looked up through the tangle of her hair at the occupant of the house.

Chapter Two

A MAN IN his shirt sleeves stood in the doorway, his dark hair falling in untidy curls about his lean, bony face. His *frowning* face. Ellis tried to straighten up but lost her balance again when she put her weight on her foot, which she seemed to have twisted when the door opened. This time he took a firm grasp on her shoulders and steadied her. That was when she noticed that his hands were stained with blue ink.

"Please," she said, in a scratchy voice. "Please, let me inside. He will find me, and if he does it will be the end of me."

The words didn't make much sense, but perhaps her torn clothing and dishevelment, along with the stark terror in her eyes, were enough to convince him.

He stepped back and, with an arm about her to hold her up, ushered her inside. At the same time, he turned his head, his gaze sweeping across the dark expanse of the forest. "He?" he repeated.

There was a chair nearby and when she didn't answer he helped her into it. Then he closed the heavy door and threw the bolt.

It was the most comforting sound Ellis had ever heard.

The house was cool and almost as gloomy as the forest. Her brief inspection showed a long, narrow table upon which sat a bowl of flowers, their perfume scenting the air. Natural light came from an open door to her left, while stairs adorned with a red carpet runner led upward into the shadows. The patterned Turkish rug beneath her feet felt wonderfully soft on her abused flesh, and the chair was so comfortable she was tempted to close her eyes.

"*Who* is trying to find you?"

Startled, her attention returned to her rescuer. During her five years at Breamore, she had grown used to the musical Welsh accent. Most of the people on the estate were of local origin, and hearing that lilt in his voice now made her long to trust him, despite having no reason to do so.

But she didn't know him. What if he was one of Theo's allies, and handed her over as soon as she gave her name? She stared up into his bright, hazel eyes and knew she couldn't risk it.

He must have read her doubts in her face because he leaned toward her and said quietly, "You can trust me."

As she stared back, she reminded herself that trust was simply too dangerous. "My coach was waylaid," she said. "In the forest. Highwaymen. I ran away but I think they are following me. I can't let them find me."

"They can't hurt you here," he said in that reassuring voice. "This house has protected its inhabitants since the 1400s, so believe me when I tell you, you are safe at Hawthorne Lodge."

She very much wanted to believe it. To believe *him*. There was something genuine about him. Again she asked herself: Could she tell him the truth? But the thought had barely formed in her head when there came the pounding of a fist on the front door. Ellis gave a squeak and jumped violently, her hand pressed to her chest where her heart was trying to escape.

"Open up!" a voice growled, and she recognized one of Theo's minions.

The man with the hazel eyes already had her up out of her chair, his strong grip maneuvering her toward the room from which light spilled. "In here." The pounding came again, with more cries demanding he "Open up," but he paused long enough to stare down into her face and say, "Can you be as quiet as a mouse, *cariad?*"

He waited for her jerky nod before he closed her inside.

Frozen to the spot, Ellis listened to his footsteps move away and then the outer door opening. When she heard Theo's voice she gasped and sank to her knees on the floor. It took a moment for the pounding of her heart to quiet enough for her to hear properly again, but by then the conversation had dropped to a murmur. The lilting cadences of the man with the ink-stained hands soothed her despite her terror, but whatever he said did not please Theo, who began to argue. Words like "I demand" and "must find her" did not help her shaking hands as she pressed them to her mouth to stifle her cries.

And yet, despite her dread, Ellis did not want Theo to find her like this. On her knees as if she were pleading for her life. She had more pride than that. With the help of a chaise longue covered in red velvet, she pulled her aching body upright and stood. Her ankle and her head hurt but not too badly. If she had to then she would run again.

She moved toward the window and carefully peeped out. It overlooked the garden she had noticed earlier, and although it was empty apart from the peacock preening on the top of the wall, she could see across the fields to the edge of the forest where a small band of horsemen were gathered. Had Theo followed her from the coach? Or was he searching the general area in the hope of finding her?

If he forced his way into the house, she needed a way to escape him. The window was just large enough that she could climb through and out into the garden, but when she tried the latch, she found it was either locked or too stiff for her to move. Frustrated, she turned, searching for something to use to force it open.

Behind her was a large desk covered in a mess of papers. She took a step closer, thinking to search the drawers in case there was something she could use in there. If worst came to worst, she might find a weapon to use against Theo.

Instead, her eyes fixed on the papers, and her eyes widened.

Drawings. There were sketches everywhere. Some had been created using pencil or charcoal, while others were in ink. Quite a few of them had emphatic lines slashed through them, as if the artist did not think them good enough, while others had been spared. Her eyes widened even more as she took them in. She shuffled the pages about. They all depicted women. Women in various poses, some modest and others far from it. One rendition in ink caught her attention, and Ellis found she could not look away.

The woman was smiling coyly, and she was naked. At least she was naked from the waist up. That would not be so shocking, Ellis had seen many famous paintings of naked women. But they were not like this. She, the woman, had covered her full breasts with her hands, but not very well. Or at least . . . was she covering them or offering them to the artist, or whoever it was standing in front of her? Ellis realized then that the woman's smile wasn't just coy.

It was an invitation.

Did this explain the ink on her rescuer's fingers? Was *he* the artist? It seemed very likely that he had fashioned this erotic representation. Now she looked more closely she could see the care he had taken to capture the expression on the woman's face, and the shape and fullness of her breasts. The detail of a lock of hair curling over her shoulder.

It was more than erotic. It was intimate. A warm tremble started deep in her belly. Ellis might have been standing and observing the scene, but she realized she didn't just want to be an observer. She wanted to step into the picture. She wanted to *be* that fearless woman offering herself to the man who stood before her, invisible and out of sight.

Her distraction had only lasted a few moments, but now the voices beyond the room were suddenly louder. Her head jerked up, and she forgot the lascivious drawings and prepared herself for Theo bursting into the room to confront her. Ellis would protest, she would fight him, and she would continue to do so even as he dragged her outside and rode off with her.

Could she tell him she had changed her mind and would marry him after all? That would give her more time to plan another escape. Would he believe her though? Would Theo think it simpler and more practical to snuff out her life once and for all? Her chaotic thoughts raced around in her head like mice being chased by a cat, squeaking and squealing, running for their lives.

Outside there was an angry protest, and she stopped breathing. Any moment now, any moment.

But as the time ticked by, nothing more happened. The sounds beyond the room faded, and then she heard horses galloping away. A glance at the window showed the band of men she had seen earlier turning back into the forest.

Could they be . . . were they leaving?

Ellis's fingers ached as she clung to the edge of the desk just to keep herself upright, and it was only when her head began to spin that she remembered to take a breath. The door gave a soft click as it opened.

The man with the wild curls narrowed his hazel eyes when he saw her standing by his desk. She noticed how his gaze darted to the array of artwork before he spoke.

"You are safe. They're gone." He said it with an air of satisfaction.

"G-gone?"

"I convinced them you were not here. Or perhaps it was the mention of my uncle that persuaded them." He was watching her curiously. "They did not look like highwaymen. They said they were searching the area around the forest for a woman, but they would not say why or who she was. When I asked, they informed me it was none of my business."

Her head began to spin more than ever, darkness flickering at the edges of her vision, and the next thing she knew, she was lying prone on the red velvet chaise longue and he was stooped over her, chafing her cold hands in his. Dazedly her gaze slid over him, noting the way his shirt was untied at his throat, and how the white linen contrasted nicely with his olive skin. The sleeves were rolled up from lean forearms with a smattering of dark hair, and of course his ink-stained fingers holding hers.

He watched her carefully, his bright eyes seeming to catalogue her just as she was assessing him. "One of them was a gentleman, or what passes for it anyway. Will you tell me why you are running away from them?"

Could she tell him? She knew she had to tell him something, just enough to let him agree to allow her to stay here until it was safe to leave. For all she knew Theo might be outside, watching and waiting.

"I thought they were highwaymen. I'm s-sorry. I cannot think why anyone else would want to stop my coach. They had pistols and fired shots. My . . . my coachman ran away. I was on my way to my mother when I was set upon."

She tried not to think of Breamore and sweet, adorable Archie, her dear husband and her dear friend. Dead, while his love, Elijah, wept inconsolably at his bedside. At least Elijah was safe. She had sent him away, protesting, before Archie was cold. She had already known what Theo was planning. Greedy, ambitious Theodore, cousin to Archie, who wanted it all. And now the only thing standing in his way was Ellis.

How could she explain to this man, this stranger, the deal she had struck with Archie? No, the truth was not worth the risk.

"Where does your mother live?" he asked, still watching her with that penetrating gaze, as if he could draw the story out of her by sheer force of will.

"In London." That was true at least. "My father is dead."

"Your father?"

"He was a curate. He died when his horse fell." She did not have to pretend at the grief that stark statement brought with it. Ellis still missed him.

His nod was thoughtful as he processed the information.

"London," he said with a frown. "Have you somewhere else you can go? Somewhere nearby?"

She shook her head. Her mother was in London and so was her sister Sophia. Her elder sister, Catherine, was widowed and living in a castle in the north. She supposed she could go to London, but the thought of setting out again, with Theo scouring the countryside for her, did not seem like a sensible plan. She needed somewhere safe to hide, until Theo had given up or gone away, and then she could make her way to the capital.

"I lost everything when my coach was stopped. I suppose I can write to my mother in London, and perhaps she will send me the fare for the journey?"

His thumbs were stroking the backs of her hands, and it felt calming. Mesmerizing. Her tense body began to relax. "That sounds like a good idea. In the meantime, you are welcome to stay here," he said. "My servants are away at the village fair, but they will return soon."

She swallowed. "Thank you."

A small smile flitted over his mouth and was gone. "I am not sure you have told me the entire truth, madam. Your 'highwayman' may come back—he does not seem like the sort to give up easily—but if he does, I will send him off again. And remind him this is Wales, where one does not enter another man's home unless invited."

"I heard him shouting," she said.

He smiled. "Yes, he shouted and blustered, while I did my best impression of an arrogant lord interrupted from his work."

His *work*? Her thoughts were diverted despite her fears. Were those saucy images his work? She wasn't sure what that meant, but it didn't seem to matter. Ellis felt safe here, safer than she had felt since Theo had arrived at Breamore.

Suddenly she was so very tired, her escape through the forest and her wildly see-sawing emotions catching up with her. Her eyes began to close.

He squeezed her hands gently, his voice as soft as a lullaby. "Rest, *cariad*," he said. "I will be here if you need me."

Chapter Three

O WEN COULDN'T KEEP his eyes off her. She was the most beautiful woman he had ever seen, and he had an eye for beauty. It wasn't just physical beauty either, but the way her emotions shone from her dark eyes and her mouth tilted at the corners as if it was made to smile, even if she wasn't smiling now. It was a face that caught and held his attention.

He shot a glance at his desk and the sketches resting on top and wondered if she had seen them. It occurred to him they would hardly inspire trust in a lone, frightened woman. But she had said nothing, so perhaps they had gone unnoticed.

Before he had been interrupted by her arrival at his door, he had been sitting at his desk, glaring at his latest efforts. His most recent model, Merrily, a young woman from the village with a sweet, innocent smile, had turned out to be a perfidious creature. She had certainly fooled Owen, and he did not consider himself someone who was easily fooled. Merrily had won his confidence, and then she had stolen his drawings of her, as well as his purse.

When he went looking for her, Merrily's father had informed him that his daughter believed her future lay in London rather than in this out of the way place. Once she had discovered her smile and her naked body could be used to make money, she had begun to imagine a fortune awaited her. Owen doubted it, but if anyone could manipulate her way under a man's guard then it was Merrily.

He felt foolish to have trusted her and told himself he would not be so gullible again. He also knew it wouldn't be long before his publisher, Hugh Madrigal, began sending him stern reminders that he had yet to fulfill his quota of artistically rendered naked ladies.

Recently there had been many more subscribers signing up for his books than Hugh knew what to do with, which in one way was flattering, but in another increased the pressure on Owen. With the jump in sales, Hugh was already talking about the new series of drawings that Owen was meant to be producing, which was all very well, but Owen did not crave fame and fortune. Yes, he enjoyed using his talent, and the money came in handy whenever he felt like he was encroaching on his uncle's generosity. Owen had been a child when his parents died, leaving him nothing but debts, and Uncle Steven had taken him in and treated him like his own. His uncle had ensured he was now free of debt, but the thought of relying upon him for everything made Owen uncomfortable.

It was true that, once upon a time, Owen had dreamed of being a famous portrait painter, with eager sitters queuing at his door and the art world marvelling at his work. His one attempt to enter the Royal Academy of Arts had met with sneers and derision, and from then on he'd resolved to turn his back on what he considered a pompous, condescending, and outmoded institution. He and Hugh Madrigal had begun their association shortly afterward, and for years Owen had been perfectly happy with his situation. His books of drawings sold well, people liked them and wanted more. There weren't many other artists who could say that.

So it wasn't waning popularity that had kept him up last night. It was that he lacked a model, had an imminent deadline, and was struggling with his work. He had also begun to feel, even before Merrily, that his creative spark was dimming. He probably needed to try something different, but he also knew Hugh Madrigal would not thank him for it. At least the problem of a new model may have been solved. This woman had landed on his doorstep in the most serendipitous way, and although Owen wasn't a great believer in fate, or of things moving mysteriously, this seemed too auspicious to ignore.

A shiver of excitement ran through him. She was *perfect*. He was already thinking about how he could pose her for the best effect, which was hardly fair of him, not after what she had told him about highwaymen. And he had seen for himself she was in some kind of danger. Owen wasn't a fool, and he suspected she didn't want to tell him the truth for a reason, but for now it suited him to pretend not to notice. Did that make him a selfish, calculating fellow? Or was he just being a polite, understanding gentleman?

A bit of both perhaps.

Cautiously, Owen rose from the chaise longue. The woman had fallen asleep and was breathing softly, her body relaxed. Her black gown was torn. Was she a widow or in mourning for the father she had mentioned? From the state of her hands and stockings she must have fought her way through brambles. She had lost a shoe and there were leaves and twigs adorning her tangled hair. That part of her story must be true at least—she really had been running for her life.

He looked down at his sleeping guest and admitted that her mysterious circumstances only heightened his interest in her. A beautiful stranger suddenly appearing on his doorstep. He was intrigued and fascinated and filled with the desperate desire to start work. How long since he had felt like that? Of course, the question was: Would his mysterious guest be willing to pose for him?

Would she be willing to remove her clothing?

His cock twinged at the thought of her naked, which was wrong on so many levels that he groaned softly and strode over to his desk and sat down. He could hear her quiet breathing as she slept. As soon as Joan, his housekeeper, returned from the village, he would ask her to arrange a bath and bed for her. And if she wanted to leave in the morning, then he would send her on her way.

Although that would be very disappointing.

He was annoyed with himself for not asking her name while she was conscious. He'd been too focused on her beautiful face with its hint of vulnerability, and her soft, husky voice and his own need to draw her. Now Owen surveyed the earlier drawings laid out before him and, whereas moments ago he had been trying to tell himself they weren't too bad, all he could see now were the mistakes and obvious lack of emotion. They were poor efforts, and he could do much, much better. In sudden decision, he pushed them aside and set a new, blank page in front of him. Then he closed his eyes and considered the vision in his mind. When he opened them again, he began to draw with swift, practiced strokes of his pencil.

Even as the image took form in front of him, he could tell this was something special. This was one of those rare times when he was able to sink entirely into his work, losing himself in the desire for perfection he had pursued since he was a mere boy. Now, at eight and twenty, he was still pursuing it. Not that the subscribers complained when he didn't achieve it. Perhaps they weren't as fussy as Owen. As far as he was aware everyone else was perfectly happy with his work. It was just Owen who strived for the impossible.

He was so focused, so lost in his creation, that it was only when he heard his servants returning that he came back to himself. He wasn't even sure how long he had been engrossed in his task, but the light in the room had dimmed significantly as the summer evening had turned to night. The sleeping woman seemed to become aware of the sounds too, because she had begun to stir.

Quickly, Owen reached to cover the sketch, only to pause as he stared down at it and really saw it as a whole for the first time, rather than a series of parts of that whole. It was full of movement and emotion, and better than anything he had done in a very long time. The woman looked out at him, her eyes wide and wild, while her tangled hair framed her face. Her gown was torn at the shoulder, and she was holding it together with one elegant hand. Her stockings were smudged and ripped, and as she stood at the edge of the forest she appeared to be on the verge of fleeing.

It was strong and evocative, and Owen was delighted with it.

The woman stirred again, making a sound, and hastily he covered the drawing. She would think him a peeping Tom if she saw it, and he didn't want that. He would never hurt her, he was not that sort of man, but he wanted her to trust him. And he was selfish enough to know she represented a chance for him to more than fulfill his commitment to Hugh Madrigal and his list of devotees.

There was a tap on the door, and when it opened Joan was there, frowning at him.

"This house is as dark as a tomb," she declared. "You've been daydreaming again, haven't you, sir?"

His housekeeper liked to call Owen's artistic endeavors "day-dreaming" and at this moment she was probably right. He *had* been caught up in a dream. Before he could answer, the woman on the chaise longue gave a gasp and sat up. With her wild hair and torn dress, she was a startling sight, and Joan stared at her as if she were a ghost. At the same time, the woman looked about at her unfamiliar surroundings and appeared to be about to flee.

Joan's eyes narrowed. "And who is this? Has she been dragged through a hedge backward?"

Owen got hastily to his feet and reached out a calming hand toward the woman. "Please, don't be afraid. This is my house-keeper, Joan. She will take care of you."

Joan approached, hands on hips. "A bath, I am thinking," she said, with a questioning glance at her master.

"If you would be so kind," Owen agreed with relief. "This

lady will be staying with us until she can make other arrangements."

The woman didn't argue, and despite the fading light he could see an expression of relief on her face. It was Joan who said, "And does the lady have a name, sir?"

Owen floundered, but luckily he didn't have to admit his lack of manners.

"Ellis," said his damsel in distress. "My name is Miss Ellis Mallory."

Something about the name struck a long-ago memory, but he didn't have time to pursue it. Joan was already shuffling Miss Ellis Mallory out of the room, fussing like a mother hen. By now she had seen the ravages of the forest on Ellis and was talking about seeing to her hurts with lotions and ointments.

Joan glanced back at Owen from the door. "Supper will be a little late," she said, "but I have a feeling you will not mind."

Owen smiled. "I don't mind at all."

He heard the two of them crossing the hall to the stairs, with Joan calling for hot water to fill the bathtub. Thank God for Joan. His housekeeper had been with him since he'd first come to live here at Hawthorne Lodge. Before that, she had been a servant in his uncle's house, so she knew his family well. She might call his work daydreaming, but she had always encouraged him despite his uncle's head shaking at his nephew's chosen career.

"If you're going to paint, then paint landscapes for God's sake!" Uncle Steven had roared at him more than once. "At least there'd be less chance of you being arrested, boy!"

Owen smiled at the memory. No matter how often he explained to his uncle that he had a growing audience for his work, and that just because he didn't exhibit at the Academy in London, it did not mean he wasn't a "proper" artist, his uncle refused to believe it. All the same, he supported Owen, and always had. Ever since his uncle took him on as a child, he had always known he could depend upon the elderly viscount and had never felt a lack of either love or care. When Owen had declared he wanted to be an artist, his uncle had grumbled and then offered him Hawthorne Lodge, so that he could live in the quiet countryside and find his muse.

Owen had never been blessed by that mythical creature who could inspire him to great artistic heights, but he was happy to draw naked ladies posing while he waited.

With the household once more in the efficient hands of Joan, and his lady in distress being safely cared for, Owen breathed a sigh of relief. It was quite dark now, and he lit a lamp before he returned to his desk to examine his latest creation. It was good, very good.

Miss Mallory was a damsel in distress with secrets, perhaps dangerous secrets if the men at the door were anything to go by. He had not recognized them but then he kept to himself, rarely mingling with his neighbors. One of the men had looked as if he was prepared to push past Owen and rampage through his house to find Miss Mallory, but Owen's mention of his uncle, with his powerful political friends, had been enough to put him off. There was no reason to assume they would return. And if they were searching around the forest then there were plenty of other properties to comb through.

Instinctively, Owen knew that if he insisted that Miss Mallory tell him her secrets, she might well run off. And he didn't want that. He wanted to keep her here at Hawthorne Lodge as long as she would agree to stay. Yes, he was selfish, and he felt a pang of guilt for that, but at the same time he reminded himself that he had taken her into his home. It could not hurt to make use of her while she was here.

Owen wanted Ellis Mallory to consent to pose for him. He needed her. She just might be his muse. Although he had scoffed at that term often enough, he was definitely inspired by her. Right now, he could only guess at what beauty lay beneath her torn clothing, but he wanted to *know*. He wanted to draw her and paint her and immortalise her.

He felt almost feverish as he imagined the various positions he could ask her to assume. But . . . his excitement waned . . . would she agree? She was frightened and alone and it would be unconscionable to use her for his own benefit. What if he offered to pay her? She was obviously in need of help, and as she had lost everything in her encounter with the "highwaymen," she would need money to find her way to London where her mother lived. Owen always paid his models, so it was no hardship for him to pay Ellis Mallory.

The plan was a good one and would benefit them both. Now all he needed to do was persuade his unexpected guest to agree to it.

Because this woman had sparked something inside him. Lit a flame that had almost gone out over the past year. And now he needed to do everything in his power to keep it burning.

Chapter Four

JOAN HAD LIT a candle and, after instructing the servants to bring hot water, now carried the light before her, banishing the shadows on the stairs and in the upper part of the house. The windows, apart from the one that looked out onto the garden downstairs, were small and would let in little light during the day. As Ellis had suspected when she first saw it, the building must once have been a fortress in the days when raids and fighting were common on the border. Now it was a gentleman's home, with touches of color and comfort, but still strong enough on the outside to withstand Theo's bullying.

Joan was talking in a friendly way. Ellis tried to pay attention, but despite her sleep, her body ached and the scratches she had almost forgotten about had begun to sting again. She realized she was still wearing one slipper and bent down to remove it.

Curiously Joan watched her.

"I expect you are his lordship's new model," she said with a lift of her eyebrows, as if she knew that wasn't the case but was fishing for information. She had fair hair neatly tied back at her nape and dark watchful eyes, and from the lack of lines on her face, Ellis thought she was a great deal younger than the housekeeper at Breamore.

"Model?" Ellis asked, straightening up.

"He has been on the watch since the last one left. I believe some artists can draw without using a model, but his lordship prefers to draw from life. He is very good, and he pays well. You won't be sorry."

Ellis sorted through the information Joan had given her, and one piece stood out. "His *lordship*?" she repeated, unable to hide her surprise. Although the man's voice and mannerisms had suggested an educated Welshman, the ink on his hands had made her think he was more likely to be an artisan than an aristocrat.

"He is Lord Lyndhurst, and Hawthorne Lodge is his home. Or rather, it is his uncle's country house. His uncle is Viscount Hawthorne and an active member of Parliament. A very important man."

Which explained why Lord Lyndhurst's mention of his uncle had made Theo less inclined to force his way into Hawthorne Lodge. Ellis tried to find some memory of those names, only to fail. She wondered if she should have given Lord Lyndhurst her real name and title after all. She may have done so, if she had not been worried that when it was discovered who she was, he might decide to hand her over to Theo for money or some favor.

It had been a hard lesson, but when Archie had died she had learned it. A great many people were willing to turn their coats if it was to their own advantage.

"Are you saying that Lord Lyndhurst is an artist?" Ellis remembered the drawings on the desk, the half-naked woman doing a very bad job of hiding her breasts in her hands as she offered a coy smile.

"Yes, he is, and a very talented one," Joan said, as if daring her to argue otherwise.

"It is unusual, is it not? For a lord to be an artist?" But then some of the upper classes were more than a little eccentric. Perhaps Lord Lyndhurst was happy to wile his days away drawing women in various states of undress.

"I suspect you are right," was all Joan said. She gave Ellis a searching look. "If you are not his new model, then who are you, if I may be so bold?"

"I-I was chased by highwaymen," Ellis stammered. "In the forest. The coach overturned and I ran away and found this house. Lord Lyndhurst gave me shelter."

Joan's dark eyes narrowed with suspicion. "Highwaymen? I have never heard of such a thing. Are you sure?"

Ellis had no intention of telling this woman the truth. "They fired shots and frightened my groom," she said, hoping that was the end of it.

"Did they indeed!" Joan stared at her doubtfully. "I will send someone out to see what has become of your coach, Miss Mallory. We will get to the bottom of this."

Ellis hoped Theo's men weren't still lurking in the area, and that Rowan had escaped unharmed. She wanted to tell Joan not to bother, but that would raise the woman's suspicions even more, so she said nothing.

Joan continued to lead the way down the corridor while Ellis followed, head full of her own concerns. She still felt a little dizzy from her escape in the forest and her impromptu sleep on the chaise longue, and it was quite strange to be following this woman with her candle when earlier today she had been in the familiar surroundings of Breamore. It was as if her life as the Duchess of Breamore had been a dream . . . or perhaps *this* was the dream.

The shadows wavered around them as Joan opened a door and stepped back to allow Ellis entry. She barely had time to notice that the space was decorated in light colors, different from the dark panelling of her state suite in Breamore, when several servants arrived. With silent efficiency, they set down a metal hip bath and began to fill it with buckets of steaming water. When they were done, Joan closed the door once more. She had already lit a lamp and drawn the curtains on the night, and now the room seemed cozy and safe.

"I'm sure you are longing for a hot bath. Here, let me." Before Ellis could speak, the other woman was unbuttoning her gown, fussing at the tears in the cloth and the dirty stains that showed up even on the dark color.

Before she became a duchess, Ellis and her sisters had tended to their own wardrobe; even at their cousin's house in London they had not had their own maid. But over the past five years she had become so used to the ministrations of servants that she hardly noticed them anymore. Suddenly she felt a terrible wave of homesickness for Breamore and Archie and dear sweet Elijah, and it was only with difficulty that she swallowed back her tears.

Joan tut-tutted as more evidence of her escape became clear. "I will fetch some salve when you are clean," she said practically. She added some scent to the water, swirled it about, and then left Ellis to her ablutions.

The water was so delicious that for a moment Ellis simply lay, boneless, allowing herself to float pleasurably. She could hear voices in the house now as the servants resumed their duties, but they seemed far away. Ellis drifted. As she had run through the forest, she had tried very hard to push away all that she was leaving behind, but now those recollections rose up in suffocating waves.

Before Archie had died, her life had been aimless and comfortable, the household run by trusted servants, and she had been able to spend her days doing very much as she pleased. Her marriage may not have been the sort of marriage she had once imagined herself making, but she was grateful to Archie for all he had given her. When she thought of her eldest sister Catherine and her old, unpleasant husband, the Duke of Wellesley, she was even more grateful for Archie.

It was after Catherine had snared her old duke that their mother had decided that all her daughters must marry dukes, and she had been prepared to wait for however long it took to see her ambition realized. Ellis was young at the time of Catherine's marriage, a child of fifteen, too young to be introduced to society. An introvert and a dreamer, Ellis was quite happy to shut herself away. But she could not escape her fate forever. Once Sophia was married off, yes to *another* duke, Ellis was thrust into the spotlight.

She hadn't enjoyed it. London society was not kind. The people she met had a hard, superficial glitter that repelled her. She would have preferred to stay in her room and lose herself in her books, but she was not given a choice. Her mother insisted she make her appearance at balls and parties, while people stared at her and whispered about her, until she found a duke who was single and needed a wife.

It was on her nineteenth birthday that she met Archie, the son of the Duke of Breamore. Archie had just arrived in London from his family estate on the Welsh border, and as fate would have it, he was in search of a wife.

At least that was what he had told her when they had danced together that first time. She had confessed that she was not much of a dancer and in fact preferred to spend her time reading and escaping into the world of her imagination. If it was up to her, she had blurted out, she would be at home now instead of trying to be vivacious and interesting with people she did not know and did not like.

She had said a great deal during that first dance, the words spilling out of her as she spoke of her true feelings in a way she had never dared to do before and which would have horrified her mother. But there was something very authentic about Archie, despite his fashionable clothes and dandyish air.

She had felt as if she could tell him anything, even as the warm laughter in his eyes turned to sympathy. He had seemed to understand her feelings perfectly. During subsequent meetings they had become friends, and one day he had asked if she would listen to *his* story. It was a secret, but as she had trusted him, he was trusting her. That was when she learned Archie had a lover, a man called Elijah, but it was not possible for two men to spend their lives together, at least not openly. He needed to at least assume the trappings of a legal marriage to enable him to inherit from his ailing father. His cousin Theo was an ambitious and ruthless sort of person and would seek to make trouble if he learned Archie's marriage was not as it should be. Theo had already voiced his suspicions about Archie's tastes to Archie's father, but thankfully the duke was not inclined to listen to him.

At first Ellis was a little shocked by his confidences, but she soon put that behind her. Archie was so nice, and she wished him every happiness with Elijah and sympathized with his need to keep such a secret from the world. It was rather like one of the novels she enjoyed, although she had yet to read one where a man fell in love with another man. The idea had opened a completely new realm for her, and she realized how insular her life had been.

During their next meeting, Archie took her aside and asked if Ellis would be willing to marry him. Of course, it would be a marriage in name only, but he would see she received a generous allowance, and she would be free to live her own life. She could even take lovers . . . if she was discreet.

Ellis had blushed at that. The idea of taking a lover was not one she had ever spoken of aloud, although she had dreamed of a man who would hold her and kiss her and give her the sort of pleasure she read about in some of her more indelicate books.

In fact, only that morning her mother had been asking her what she was doing wrong because Archie should have proposed to her by now. His offer came at just the right time. She could marry a man destined to be the Duke of Breamore and please her mother, as well as help Archie to find his own happiness. No elderly husband to deal with, as was the case with Catherine, no being involved in society gossip like Sophia, who often seemed to be looking anxiously over her shoulder.

It was a perfect solution, and she happily accepted.

The wedding was like a fairytale with Archie insisting on seeing to every detail to make it so, and if his smiles to Elijah hinted that he wished it was the two of them tying the knot rather than he and Ellis, well, she could sympathize. She was looking forward to her future, to living at Breamore and doing as she pleased.

What she had not expected to feel was lonely.

Oh, there was plenty to do at her new home. When the duke died and Archie inherited the title, Ellis became a duchess with her own suite of rooms and more books than she knew what to do with. She could ask for any book she wanted, and some of the titles that arrived from the printer in London were risqué to say the least. Meanwhile Archie and his lover, Elijah, were wonderful companions and dear friends, and their days were full of laughter. But the nights . . . Archie and Elijah had each other, and she could see how deeply they were in love, how much they desired each other. But Ellis was a young woman with her own desires, and her reading had given her an idea of how her life might be, if she found the right lover.

Archie did not notice her sadness, he was too happy himself, but Elijah did. In his gentle voice he reminded her that she was entitled to take a lover. There were a great many handsome men to choose from, he'd added with a wink, and Ellis had smiled back and promised to cast her eye over them. But she was not wholly comfortable acting in such a brash way. It was easier in fiction. Real life seemed awkward, and she had had no practice at all, unlike Sophia who flirted as if it was second nature to her. She thought about asking her sister to give her some lessons but then Sophia would ask questions, and she didn't want to risk Sophia discovering the truth. Which meant she had still not chosen anyone by the time Archie had died and her life had changed so drastically.

Now Ellis sighed, sinking lower in the warm water, and pushed aside her sadness. She reminded herself that she might be in a house full of strangers whom she could not trust, but at least she was safe. For now, anyway. Lord Lyndhurst had sent Theo away, and he had said she could remain here until she was able to make her way to London. She had time to gather her thoughts and consider her future.

Her mind circled back to the drawings scattered over Lord

Lyndhurst's desk, and that one drawing in particular. The half-naked woman.

She reached down into the water to cover her own breasts, allowing the soft flesh to overflow her fingers, and then brushing her thumbs over her rosy nipples. If felt forbidden. Naughty. There was a tingle through her nerve endings, and the sensation was so pleasant she continued to stroke herself. Soon her nipples turned into hard little buds, and the tingling sensation was echoed between her thighs. She couldn't help but give a gasp of pleasure.

What had Joan said? That Lord Lyndhurst needed a new model, someone to pose for his indelicate drawings? Ellis felt the warmth between her legs build. Could she agree to be that person? It would give her a reason to stay here until she made a solid plan for her future. For too long she had wanted someone to hold her, touch her, kiss her. Her body was eager for a lover's ministrations, while at the same time her heart ached for the sort of closeness she had seen between Archie and Elijah.

Her narrow escape from Theo made her think she should not wait any longer. She needed to act, find the lover she had promised herself for five years, and enjoy him. Enjoy her life. Because who knew what her future might hold?

She was so deep in her thoughts that she jumped when there was a brisk tap on the door.

But it was only Joan. The housekeeper bustled in and set a small case upon the bed and began to sort through it, setting aside various small bottles. Another servant followed her in, a plump pretty girl with tawny hair, who Joan introduced as Polly.

"Polly will look after you while you're here," Joan added, as if there was no doubt in anyone's mind about Ellis staying. She didn't argue. It seemed as if the decision had been taken out of her hands.

Without further ado, Polly knelt by the tub and began to wash Ellis's hair, avoiding the bump from when the coach overturned. Ellis closed her eyes and let herself enjoy the sensation of the girl's strong hands on her scalp and the flowery scent of the soap.

Joan's voice from across the room drifted over her. "Polly, when you are finished, find Miss Mallory one of Merrily's gowns. Miss Mallory will be dining with his lordship."

Startled from her fugue, Ellis sat up abruptly. "Dine with him?" she burst out, and then spluttered as the stinging soap and water ran into her eyes. Polly handed her a towel so that Ellis could mop her face.

"Just as well I restocked the larder," was all the housekeeper said. "Otherwise it would be thin soup and a crust of stale bread."

Polly snorted a laugh and then coughed to disguise it.

"His lordship is not a worldly man when it comes to the practical details of running a household," Joan explained to Ellis. "He is a dreamer. Just as well Polly and I are here to take care of him."

Ellis had not thought his lordship helpless when he had re-fused to allow Theo into his house, but she said nothing as Polly urged her from the bath and wrapped her in a drying cloth. Seating her on a stool, Polly then began briskly to dry her hair, while Joan came to examine her hurts. She was applying a sweet-smelling unguent on the scratches on her hands, when Polly slipped out of the room only to return with a garment in her arms.

"Will this do?" she said and held it up.

It was a gown made of an abundance of turquoise satin that shone and rippled in the candlelight, while the elbow length sleeves were trimmed with delicate white lace. It was beautiful, but was it suitable to wear to dine with a gentleman she hardly knew? Before she could ask the question, Polly was helping her step into the gown, and fastening up the ties and hooks. Once that was done, the two women stepped back and stood close together, silently observing the effect.

Joan and Polly exchanged glances, their eyebrows raised. What did *that* mean? Was the dress not flattering? Disappointed, Ellis turned to the looking glass. Her eyes widened. She looked . . . ethereal. The sea-colored gown made her think of a mermaid come to dry land. But there was nothing otherworldly about the way the gleaming cloth clung to her hips, or how her breasts were barely contained by the bodice, her abundant white flesh spilling over in a manner that was almost indecent.

"Whose gown did you say this was?" she asked in a breathless voice.

"Merrily's," Joan responded. "His lordship's last model. She never wore it. The color did not suit her." She waved a dismissive hand. "Don't worry about her, she's gone."

Polly had laid out stockings and slippers on the bed, and now she finished dressing Ellis. Her hair was still damp, but when she pointed it out, Polly shrugged as if that was immaterial. "Let's leave it down. His lordship won't mind. It is an informal meal, after all, isn't it?"

She exchanged another glance with Joan, and they both smiled as if they shared a secret.

Ellis opened her mouth to protest, to say she was too tired or too overwhelmed by all that had happened and could not possibly go downstairs in a borrowed dress with her hair down. But she didn't. The truth was she wanted to dine with Lord Lyndhurst.

All her life Ellis had put herself in the shoes of her heroines, imagining herself doing bold and daring deeds. But the only brave thing she had ever done was marry Archie.

Now everything had changed, and her life had become very precarious. Who knew what would happen to her next? She did not want any regrets when the end came, she wanted to live life to the full. She had spent enough time in the wings, waiting.

Ellis wanted to step out onto the stage.

Chapter Five

"I S THIS ENTIRELY necessary?" Owen waved a hand over the small table by the fireplace, with the single candle making the silver cutlery and crystal glassware gleam. It was all very . . . intimate.

Owen had blurted out to Joan his hopes and dreams when she had visited his study while Miss Mallory was bathing. And he'd best not let his imagination stray to that during dinner! The housekeeper had wanted to tell him about a coach in the forest, and her qualms concerning their new arrival. Owen had listened, aware that this was really about Merrily and the hurt she had inflicted on him.

"I understand your concern, but Miss Mallory is exactly what I need," he had said. "Hugh Madrigal wants a new series of drawings, and she is perfect for it."

Now, despite her doubts, Joan seemed determined to help him get his wish. She straightened a fork on the table and shot him a look. "Yes, it *is* necessary. You want her to agree to be your model, don't you?"

He did, that was true.

"Then you need to woo her like a lover until she says 'yes'. You've been like a bear with a sore head since Merrily left. Polly and I only want you to be happy, my lord."

Owen ignored the "Polly and I." Although he was fully aware that his housekeeper and his maid slept in the same bed, he didn't think it was his place to make comment on it. Who was he to judge when he spent his time creating salacious artworks? He understood that Joan was in a precarious position. She didn't want him leaving Hawthorne Lodge because then she may have to leave too, and it was unlikely anyone else would be quite as sympathetic to the relationship between the two women. Keeping Owen happy was good for everyone.

"Do you think Miss Mallory is in danger?" he asked the question that had been niggling at him since Ellis arrived at his door. "In those circumstances it doesn't seem fair to persuade her to pose for me, as much as I might want her to."

"Why not? This is the ideal place for someone who is in danger. She can hide here for as long as she likes and help you in the meantime. It can be an understanding between the two of you. Why not ask her and see what she says?"

But Owen still felt uncomfortable about using Ellis Mallory's sudden arrival to his own advantage. It seemed a bit caddish to him, and Owen was no cad. He opened his mouth to argue with Joan's simplistic view, just as Miss Mallory walked into the room.

After that he couldn't say anything because he was struck dumb by the sight of her, and even when Joan gave a soft, knowing laugh, he couldn't tear his gaze away.

She was wearing something he vaguely recognized, but it was the way she wore it that caught him. Turquoise satin clung to her curves, rippling like a living thing every time she moved. Her bosom was barely confined by the bodice, spilling over in its abundance, while her dark hair was heavy and loose about her shoulders. His fingers itched to begin drawing her. It was all he could do not to rush off to his study and fetch the necessary equipment.

He became aware that she was watching him from beneath her long spiky lashes in a manner that was almost shy. It *was* shy. This was no practiced move. Ellis Mallory might be stunningly beautiful, but he suspected she was not the sort of woman to flaunt that beauty just for the effect it would have on those around her. And somehow that made Owen fall even more deeply under her spell.

He swallowed. He would have to say something. The silence had gone on for far too long, and even without looking he knew Joan would be smirking.

"Miss Mallory, please won't you be seated?"

When she didn't move, looking uncertainly at the *very* intimate setting, he held out his hand. He wasn't sure if she would accept the invitation, but she did, her hand nestling in his. No gloves, and skin that was soft and warm, her fingers quivering a little as he held them in his. And, oh God, his cock gave a definite twitch.

As she allowed him to seat her, a lock of her hair brushed against his fingers. A sweet, clean womanly scent engulfed him, and he found himself stilling, breathing her in. Surely he had never felt like this before? Owen wasn't even sure what to make of it. He hardly noticed Joan leaving the room, with a murmured, "Dinner will be served shortly," before the door closed behind her. All of his attention and every one of his senses were focused on Ellis Mallory.

He had to force himself to step away.

Once seated, Owen reached for the red wine, pouring it carefully into two goblets. The deep ruby color reflected the candlelight as he raised his glass. What should he drink to? Her beauty? His hopes for his new series of drawings? None of that seemed appropriate, so he contented himself with, "To your good health, Miss Mallory."

She did not respond, nor did she look up. Her hands were clasped together on the table before her, and she was staring down at them. He could see the white of her knuckles. He wanted to tell her she was safe, that no one could hurt her while he was here, but perhaps it was better to steer clear of that subject for now. He would help her to relax and enjoy the meal.

Owen cleared his throat and prepared to be a good host.

"I hope you are feeling more the thing now," he said, a little awkwardly. Her gaze lifted to his. Liquid brown eyes, full of secrets, tugging him down into their depths. He could stare into them forever.

"Thank you. I am feeling much better," she replied in her soft, husky voice. "You have been very kind. I am sorry to trespass on your hospitality. If you could lend me enough money for coach fare, I could leave tomorrow."

It was more of a question than a suggestion, but it was still not what he wanted to hear.

"You can stay as long as you like," he said in a no-nonsense way. "Indeed, I insist upon it. If you want to send a message to your mother, then I am happy to ensure it will be delivered, but for now I think you should stay at Hawthorne Lodge and—and recover."

Was that too autocratic? He tried to soften it. "It would be my great pleasure to be your host for as long as you wish it."

She seemed to be trying to read his thoughts. After a moment she said, "You are very kind," in a stilted voice, and began rearranging her cutlery, moving the pieces back and forth as if she was too restless to be still. "But . . . we are strangers. As much as I would like to stay . . ." She bit her lip. "Is there some way I can repay you for your hospitality?"

Owen had been taking a sip of his wine and it went down the wrong way. He coughed, holding the napkin to his lips. She had given him the perfect opening, and it was now or never. He had to speak. He could not let her slip through his fingers, he really couldn't.

He set the napkin aside. "There *is* a way in which you can repay me, Miss Mallory. Although, let me be clear, there is absolutely no obligation for you to do so."

Now her gaze was fixed on his, her restless fingers stilled. "Oh?"

"It is nothing . . . unpleasant I assure you. At least . . ." He cleared his throat again. "I am an artist. I illustrate books for a certain type of reader. They sell rather well if I do say so myself, but recently my sitter . . . my model left for greener pastures, and I find it difficult to draw without one. I wondered . . . I wondered if you would consider posing for me. It would be an entirely professional arrangement. A kindness really, and a great help to me. But of course, if you do not wish to—"

"Yes."

Her reply was so sudden he froze, staring back at her. "Yes? Did you say . . .?"

A little smile twitched at the corners of her mouth, and his cock went hard so quickly he was worried he might spill in his pantaloons.

"Yes?" he repeated, hoping to hell he had not misheard. "You *will* pose for me?"

"Yes, I would be happy to pose for you. It is the least I can do after your kindness in allowing me to stay. It would be recompense, of a sort, and then I would not feel I had to leave."

"You wouldn't have to leave anyway," he said sternly, doing his best to hide the wild joy clamoring inside him. "This would be a favor to me, and certainly not an obligation, Miss Mallory, I promise you."

She smiled again and lifted her goblet to her lips. When she had sipped and lowered it again, there was a droplet of wine on her lips. She licked it off with the tip of her tongue. It was only when her gaze sharpened on his, questioningly, that he became aware that he had groaned aloud.

"There would be nothing else involved," he said quickly, perhaps more for his benefit than hers. "Just sitting. I want you to feel perfectly safe, even if you were . . . if you agreed to be . . . if . . ."

"Naked?" she suggested, with an arch of her eyebrows. Laughter sparkled in her eyes and the corners of her lips lifted again into a real smile.

Owen knew then that he was lost. Completely and utterly.

"I saw your drawings," Miss Mallory admitted with that upward flick of her eyelashes. Her dark eyes gleamed with mischief. "I'm sorry if I shouldn't have looked, but they were difficult to ignore."

"You wouldn't be naked," he said hastily. "Well, not at first. And never, if you prefer not to remove your clothing. I do assure you a woman can look just as appealing when she is clothed."

She seemed to consider this. "Then I can agree to what you ask, or disagree if I feel so inclined . . .? We *agree* on that, Lord Lyndhurst?"

"Yes," he said earnestly, leaning forward until he was almost touching her. "I would never ask you to do anything you did not feel comfortable with, Miss Mallory. That is not my way. I may be the artist of risqué pictures, but I am still a gentleman."

She considered him a moment, before she nodded. "Thank you, Lord Lyndhurst."

"Call me Owen. Please. You are doing me a favor by posing and Lord Lyndhurst seems a bit too formal in the circumstances. We need to be comfortable with each other, if I am to . . . if I . . ." Dear God why couldn't he finish a sentence? What was wrong with him?

"Owen," she repeated quietly and put an end to his stammering.

The door opened, startling them both, and Joan and Polly entered with their meal.

Chapter Six

ELLIS SLEPT WELL in the comfortable bed, her body worn out from her escape and her mind exhausted from thinking about her future. Lord Lyndhurst—Owen—had toasted to that—"To the future." For the present she was safe, and she believed him when he had told her so. She had awoken refreshed and with a low thrum of excitement growing inside her. Last night she had agreed to pose for Owen—in all honesty she had led him down the path of asking her, but she refused to feel guilty about it.

There was something very appealing in the thought, something delicious. Giving a man permission to gaze upon her at her most intimate so that he could sketch her? It was titillating. Powerful. Freeing. She suspected some men would take advantage, but even before Owen assured her he wasn't one of those men, she had trusted him. Ellis was normally a good judge of character, and he had seemed sincere. His servants liked him, which was always a good sign. She would be safe here in Hawthorne Lodge, and she was prepared to enjoy every moment of their arrangement.

She allowed her thoughts to dwell a moment on Lord Lyndhurst. He was handsome in an unconventional manner, with his wild dark hair and serious hazel eyes in a thin, angular face. He was intense, but she liked that he was serious about his work.

There was nothing superficial about him. She could imagine herself having long conversations with him in the gardens at Breamore, arguing some point or other with him over tea, or laughing as they strolled beside the flower beds. Before her life had turned upside down.

He was exactly the sort of man she had dreamed of meeting one day.

"I want you to find someone whose company you enjoy," Archie had said, with a smile, on their wedding day. "You deserve to be happy. You have been so kind to Elijah and me. I want to see you smile, Ellis."

But she hadn't found anyone. Archie and Elijah were her dear friends, and although she'd wished she had someone to love her as deeply as Elijah did Archie, she had not wanted to take the risk of choosing just anyone and ruining their idyll at Breamore. Theo was always in the background, watching, and although the two men shrugged off her worries about him, Ellis could not be so prosaic. If Archie hadn't died, Ellis might have eventually found someone. A lover to share her bed and her private moments. Perhaps even her other half, as seemed to be the case in so many romance novels.

And now, here she was, hidden from the world, safe for the moment at least, and with a man who seemed to fit her fantasies. It was as if anything was possible.

Polly soon arrived with warm water for Ellis to wash in, and a new gown for her to wear. At first sight she thought it ordinary in comparison to the one she had worn last night. This dress was a pastel pink and the sort of thing a debutante might dress in for her coming out.

Until she held it up and saw that the cloth was transparent against the light.

Polly did not seem to think she needed a chemise or petticoat, and when Ellis stood before the looking glass, the silhouette of her body was perfectly visible against the window behind her.

She had never worn anything so daring in her life, and the

thought of strolling about in it made her hesitate.

"Are you sure . . .? Is this what Lord Lyndhurst wants me to wear?"

Polly gave her a brief, disinterested glance. "Don't you like it, miss? Merrily had no trouble wearing it for her sittings with his lordship. Half the time she took it off anyway and he drew her bare."

Ellis considered this. She told herself not to be shocked, or a little jealous of Merrily, who was so comfortable in her own skin. If Merrily had worn this gown, and if Owen wanted Ellis to wear it today, then she should not be quibbling over it.

Polly gave a sniff. "I am only obeying his lordship's instructions. If you're not happy, then you'll need to take it up with him."

Ellis *could* refuse, Owen had made it clear the choice was hers, but she found she didn't want to. If she was going to model for Owen, then she should begin as she meant to go on.

That excited humming she had noticed since she first saw the drawings increased a notch, vibrating inside her and making her skin tingle.

Polly seemed to think the conversation was over and carried on with the morning toilette. She arranged Ellis's hair loosely, ringlets dancing about her face, and a pink wreath of flowers circling her crown. She really did look like a debutante just arrived at her coming-out ball—apart from the inappropriateness of the gown. Imagine appearing in front of everyone and waltzing about in a Mayfair ballroom. She almost giggled. How shocking that would be!

Polly's eyes met hers in the glass.

The maid seemed to be waiting for her to speak, and she also looked rather tense, as if Ellis's decision was important to her. Was Lord Lyndhurst that hard a taskmaster?

"His lordship will be waiting for you to join him for breakfast," Polly said at last, sounding awkward. "We . . . that is, me and Joan, we try to make sure he has at least one good meal a day. Sometimes he forgets to eat."

"Oh." Ellis understood then. The two women were worried about Lord Lyndhurst in a purely motherly way. They wanted to do their best by him, and they wanted to please him when it came to Ellis. It was loyalty and love.

"Miss Mallory?"

Ellis gave herself a mental shake. "Yes, of course." She moved toward the door only to pause again. "Are you sure?" She gestured at herself.

Polly's smile broadened. "I am very sure, miss. You're exactly what he's been looking for. I'm sorry for your troubles in the forest, but it was a very happy day for all of us when you knocked on this door."

Breakfast was served in a small room off the dining room, and the smell of food made Ellis's stomach growl. Normally, at Breamore, she would still be lolling in bed, sipping on her hot chocolate and nibbling on toast before choosing which gown to wear and wondering what she would do to fill in the day. Perhaps a walk in the Great Park or the white garden or chatting with Elijah and practicing the latest dances with Archie. And reading. Her favorite thing of all was to lose herself in the fictional world of a book.

Now she stood in the doorway of Hawthorne Lodge in a transparent gown, about to pose for a man she barely knew, and it felt as if she had stepped into the pages of one of those novels. But instead of reading about the heroine's adventures, she was taking part in them.

Owen was sitting at the table reading a newspaper. He must have heard her because he looked up swiftly. For a moment he went still before he rose to his feet.

"Miss Mallory!" he said. "Good morning." He was such a gentleman that she couldn't help but smile. His gaze dropped down, taking in her outfit, and she could have sworn she saw the movement of his throat as he swallowed. "You look very becoming," he said, and his voice had dropped an octave.

Ellis wondered if he could see through her dress. She suspected he could, by the way in which he kept looking at her and then away again. Perhaps he was thinking of his next sketch—the composition, the colors . . . At least, she supposed so, but the faint flush on his cheeks made her wonder if he was thinking of other things as well.

The thrumming inside her had returned and was already at a low hum. She wanted to wriggle and twirl, like a child faced with a long-awaited treat.

Instead, she dropped a polite little curtsy in response to his greeting. When she saw the silver chafing dishes set out on the sideboard, she automatically went to serve herself. There was quite an array of food, and her hunger informed her that she needed to satisfy it.

Behind her she heard Owen clear his throat. "You slept well?"

"Yes. Very well, thank you." She turned to smile at him over her shoulder and a lock of hair slid from its pins into her eyes. With an embarrassed laugh she reached to push it back.

"Stop!" he shouted. "Don't move!"

Ellis froze, eyes wide, wondering what was wrong. She dared not move, but watched as Owen began frantically searching the table beneath his abandoned newspaper. With a triumphant cry he held up a sketchbook and pencil. Then he looked up at her, bright eyes narrowing.

"Can you just . . . for a moment . . . just don't move." His pencil moved incredibly quickly over the paper, his eyes flicking continuously from her to his work. "That's it," he murmured. "Yes. Stay just like that."

Ellis stood as still as she could, wondering if it was safe to breathe, but it only seemed a few moments later that Owen stopped drawing and grinned at her. As he raked his fingers back through his wild curls, he suddenly looked much younger and more carefree.

"Thank you," he said. "That was just so . . . I had to capture it. If I hadn't, then I would have regretted it." He gave a self-conscious laugh. "You can eat now."

"Oh. I-I'm glad. That you captured it," Ellis responded nervously.

As she turned back at last to fill her plate, she couldn't help but wonder what his drawing looked like. She wanted to ask him if she could see it, but then she pondered whether that was part of their deal. Did the artist share his work with his model? She brought her plate to the table and sat down. Owen poured her a cup of tea and pushed the toast rack toward her. There were little pots of butter and marmalade and strawberry jam.

"No one will ever starve in this household," Owen said wryly, as he watched her make her choices. "The problem I have is *not* to get fat."

Ellis smiled. He was far from that. With his tall frame—long legs, narrow hips, and broad shoulders—he looked a little too slim. She remembered what Polly had said and imagined him becoming so engrossed in his work at times that he forgot to eat. She imagined that Joan and Polly probably overcompensated for moments like that by offering him far more food than he needed, just so that they could see him eat.

"Do you ride? Or walk?" she asked, as she cut into a crispy slice of bacon. When he didn't answer she glanced up.

He was still watching her with that focused stare, and she tried not to let it make her feel uncomfortable. She suspected he wasn't really seeing *her* but a picture he could make with her in it.

"I ride," he said at last, seeming to pull himself back from wherever he had been. "Mostly in the early morning. And I walk during the day if the weather is clement. I find the fresh air helps the creative process."

"I walk, too," Ellis said. "At my home there are some lovely walks by the stream, and a small bridge where I can watch the fish. They were imported from—" Remembering herself, she stopped. She must not give too much away. As vast as the Breamore estate had been, he might recognize parts of it. Maybe he had been there? Although she thought that if he had ever visited, then she would remember.

There was something very memorable about Owen, Lord Lyndhurst.

In any event, he asked her no more, respecting her silence. She wondered if he had read her unease in her voice and her face—he seemed very empathetic. When she pushed her plate back and finished her second cup of tea, Ellis dabbed her lips with her napkin and saw that Owen was still watching her. He almost looked to be vibrating with anticipation for their sitting, and the idea made her want to smile.

"Are you ready?" he asked, hastily getting to his feet. "Shall we begin?"

Ellis rose, too.

His gaze dropped to her breasts, which were decently confined but perhaps he could see through the thin cloth of her bodice, because that flush rose in his cheeks again.

"Good, very good," he muttered, and quickly turned away. "Follow me, Miss Mallory."

It was the same room she had hidden in yesterday, but the chaise longue had been pulled over by the window and a chair placed before it. Owen's drawing equipment was on the seat, all ready for their session to begin. He gestured for Ellis to take the chaise longue.

Then he stood and looked at her for a few moments before he reached out a hand toward her, only to stop and say, "If I may?"

Ellis nodded, and permission given, Owen set about arranging her to his satisfaction.

Feeling his warm but impersonal hands on her body was a little disconcerting. After a moment she decided not to think of him as a man. He was an *artist*. He was posing her to represent some idea he had fixed in his mind. He probably did not even see *her*. Ellis tried to relax and make herself malleable.

When Owen finished, she was sprawled upon the chaise longue, her legs stretched out, with her feet crossed at the ankles.

Her upper body was raised, and her chin rested on her hand, with her arm bent and elbow set upon a cushion. It was a position she often enough assumed when she was reading in the conservatory at Breamore, so it was comfortable, if a little odd, to have an audience.

Owen had stepped back to run his gaze over her. "Yes," he said with satisfaction. "Hold that for as long as you can. If you need to stretch, then tell me, Miss Mallory, and I can stop for a while."

"Call me Ellis," she said. "Please."

His eyes searched hers briefly, and something in his face softened. "Ellis," he agreed.

He had another long look at her, the considering look she was beginning to recognize as his "artist's look," as if he was on a higher plane than a mere mortal, and then he reached out to rearrange a strand of her hair where it rested against her bodice. His fingers were so quick and light she hardly felt them, and yet they left behind goose bumps on her skin. She suspected her nipples tightened too, but she hoped he could not see that, although if he did she was sure he would be too gentlemanly to say so.

"Now," he said with an eager note, more to himself than her, "let us begin."

Chapter Seven

OWEN SAT DOWN and began to work. He had been dying to begin ever since she had walked into the breakfast room in that dress. He had suggested the garment to Polly this morning but had half expected Ellis to refuse to wear it. She seemed to be a respectable woman despite her travails, and the respectable women he was acquainted with would never wear anything so daring.

He was very pleased when she did.

Ellis Mallory was stunning, and he was fired with the desire to capture not just her outer beauty but the inner woman. The vulnerability and shyness he sometimes saw in her expression. The secrets in her dark eyes. His pencil flew. Her gaze was fixed on his, as if she wasn't sure where to look, but gradually she seemed to relax, and soon her stare became dreamy.

Owen paused and considered his sketch. It would do nicely for the first in this new series. What should he call it? *The Lady at Ease*, perhaps? *The Lady's Adventures*? *The Lady's Amorous Adventures*? The title would come to him. But he needed more than Ellis at rest. Hugh Madrigal's subscribers would be seeking rather more than just a beautiful woman on a chaise longue. An idea came to him. Should he ask her? She had seemed perfectly happy to go along with his suggestions so far.

Carefully he set down his pencil. "Ellis," he said quietly, "would you mind a more enticing pose?"

The dreaminess left her brown eyes, and she gave him a curious look. "Your sketches are meant to entice?" she asked, although he suspected she knew that if she had seen the ones on his desk.

But Owen needed to be frank. Honest. At least then he would know how far Ellis was willing to go as his model. They should be open with each other, without artifice.

"The gentlemen—and ladies—who purchase my books want to be aroused."

"And this is not arousing?" she asked curiously, looking down at herself. There was a hint of color in her cheeks.

"It is a—a promise of what is to come. The lady at her ease, but what else is she about to get up to? Do you see? You need to fulfil that promise." Something in her face made him add quickly, "But if you are not comfortable with that, then we will carry on as we are now. I assure you I am happy to follow your lead." He could use his imagination for something more salacious, and although he was always better at drawing from life, he rather thought with Ellis Mallory his imagination could run quite wild.

She shook her head, those ringlets dancing about her face. "No, no, I don't mind. I have never . . . that is, I would be happy to pose in whatever way you wish, Owen."

Her brown eyes were earnest, but then she licked her lips.

God. Speaking of *aroused* . . .

He moved in his chair, holding the sketchbook firmly over his lap. "Thank you," he said "I appreciate this, Ellis. And again, if you are not comfortable with any of it, then do let me know. I am not a hard, eh, taskmaster." Although he was currently hard in other areas.

She nodded with that same earnestness. "Truly, it is not much to ask. I am doing very little." She gave a faint laugh. "You are doing all of the work."

That wasn't strictly true. Owen knew a good model was like

gold, and so far he had found Ellis inspired him in a way he had not been inspired for years. Perhaps ever. Back to work, he told himself firmly.

"Can you move your hand?" he said.

"My hand . . .?" she repeated. "Where do you . . .?"

"Can I show you?"

She nodded and watched him approach. Owen looked down at her a moment, consideringly, and then reached to take her hand and place it against her chest, where her neckline dipped. "Perhaps, with your fingers just inside the bodice. As if you are thinking of touching yourself."

Her cheeks were rosy pink now, but she did as he asked, slipping her fingers inside the cloth. He arranged her a little differently and tugged the bodice down farther so that the upper globe of her breast was exposed but her nipple remained hidden. At this point he wanted to imply the temptation rather than be explicit.

He considered her again, and then went to move before stopping abruptly. "If I may?"

She nodded, and he arranged her hair so that a lock lay over her cheek, a little unkempt. As if she was flustered, maybe imagining herself with a gentleman friend. He smiled at the thought.

"What?"

"I was just thinking . . ." Why not tell her? If she knew the look he was attempting, then she would be more likely to achieve it. She had proven herself amiable to his wishes so far.

"I want you to appear as if you are dreaming of a lover. Or— no!" His voice rose in excitement as the image came to him. "Your lover is in the room, watching you. He wants you, and you want him, but you are teasing him. Tantalizing him."

It would make a wonderful series of drawings.

Her doubtful expression cleared. "Oh, I see!" She looked at him through her lashes, and his cock was getting hard again. How on earth was he going to remain professional with this woman?

Well, there was no question about it, he would just have to.

She wriggled on the sofa, her skirt hitching up to her knee, and leaned back, her hand resting against her breast, fingers slipping inside the cloth of her bodice. It was exactly what he wanted.

"Yes," he said and wondered why his voice was so hoarse. He cleared his throat again. "Yes, that's it. Stay just like that."

She smiled, pleased she had pleased him, and he almost groaned aloud.

Owen wasn't usually this easily stimulated during sittings. The opposite if anything. It was a job, and when he looked at these women, he saw merchandise Hugh Madrigal wanted to sell, rather than a flesh and blood being. Besides, having no emotional or physical interaction between himself and his model was his rule, unless he was helping her achieve the pose he wanted. And after Merrily, he really didn't want another woman to take advantage of him as she had.

So why on earth was he allowing himself to feel like this with Ellis Mallory? He told himself to for God's sake get a grip and sat down to begin the new sketch.

A smile was still lingering on her lips, and he replicated it, the image taking shape easily and quickly. The sketch was another one of his best, he already knew that. Whenever he thought he had reached an artistic pinnacle, he found himself reaching another, higher one. He looked up again, to see if he had the lock of hair correct, and found she was watching him.

"What now?" she asked, tucking her hair back behind her ear before she remembered she had to remain still. "Sorry," she whispered.

He sketched in the delicate whorls of her ear.

"Owen?"

"I . . ." He chewed on his lip. "Would you be willing to unbutton your gown a little? Remember I am looking to tantalize."

"Hmm, tantalize," she echoed thoughtfully. She slipped her sleeve down over her shoulder and onto her arm and bent her opposite arm to rest her hand upon the curve of her now bare shoulder, which had the effect of squeezing her breasts together. They looked plump and delicious, the texture of her pale skin so tempting it was agony not to touch her.

"Yes, ah, yes," he muttered, and immediately began to draw again.

After that, the morning flew by. Owen completed numerous sketches, all of them good, and they were certainly tantalizing. The final one was of Ellis seated, leaning forward, with her hand holding her loosened bodice in place. There was the sense that if she let go the cloth would fall and expose her completely. Owen worked feverishly to capture the look in her eyes. Was it a come-hither look or was he imagining that? The finished work was exactly what he had hoped for, and he was beginning to imagine a far larger series than he had first planned.

Of course, she would need to strike even more alluring poses to complete the set. He was already aware that he was pushing her into areas new to her, but she was more compliant than he had expected and hadn't pulled back or complained. Indeed, he suspected Miss Ellis Mallory was enjoying herself. Whenever he suggested something new her eyes gleamed as if he had set her a challenge she was determined to meet.

It was Owen who wondered if he would survive much more of this.

Every time he drew the shape of her smiling lips, he wanted to kiss them. Run his tongue down the arch of her throat and push aside the loosened bodice and suck upon her breasts. He wanted her thighs clamped around his hips. He wanted to be deep inside her. He wanted to hear her gasp and moan and feel her shiver with pleasure. He wanted to be the man to do all of that. It was sheer torture to keep himself in check, but he reminded himself it was a torture he was willing to undergo.

"We should eat," he said abruptly, doing his best to sound normal.

She looked a little disappointed, but refastened her gown and stood up, rearranging the cloth so that it covered her properly. She slipped her shoes back on and led the way to the door.

"What about this afternoon?" she asked hopefully, with a look over her shoulder. "Will we do this again?"

Owen knew he should say no, give himself some time to cool down, but it seemed he was completely helpless when it came to her. "If you are certain?" he tried. "You must be tired."

Her laughter teased his already raw senses. "Not at all. The opposite in fact." Then, a little uncertainly, "Can I see what you've drawn?"

"Of course," he said in surprise, "but some of the sketches may seem rough to you. I will need to do some more work to make them presentable. After that you are welcome to look at them."

She smiled again. "No one has ever drawn me. There was talk of a portrait, before . . ." She stopped and bit her lip, as if to force the words back. "Apart from my own face in a looking glass, I have never seen myself as someone else sees me. As *you* see me."

His heart seemed to still, before it began to beat furiously again.

Before he could answer, not that he knew what to say, Polly appeared and informed them, "Luncheon is ready, sir. Miss Mallory."

In the dining room, Joan and Polly were putting the finishing touches to the table. Owen stared at it with narrowed eyes. Flowers? He could not remember the last time he had a bunch of flowers before him while he ate his solitary meal. But last night there was a candle and today there were flowers on the table. This must be in honor of Ellis.

He raised a questioning eyebrow at his housekeeper, but she avoided his gaze.

"I hope you had a productive morning," she said, hands folded at her waist.

Before Owen could answer, Ellis did. "It was fun." She sat down before he could draw out her chair and reached for her napkin. Her loosened hair fell over her shoulders, and she tossed it back. "I'm starved," she informed her audience, and began to serve herself.

Owen watched her, ever curious when it came to her. She was obviously wellborn, or at least had grown up among those who were, and yet she was so unspoiled. There was no artifice to her, no game playing. She was just herself, and it felt like she was everything he had ever wanted in a woman.

He snapped out of his trance, realizing they were all looking at him. Joan smirked and Polly huffed a laugh, while Ellis smiled kindly.

"You were far away," she said. "Are you thinking of your work?"

"Something like that," he murmured as he sat down.

After that Joan and Polly left them alone, and Owen realized how famished he was. Now if only he could keep his eyes off the woman opposite him and push aside his filthy thoughts when it came to her, he might be able to eat.

Chapter Eight

"Ellis?"

Owen was speaking and she was far away. For the past three days they had been working together. Well, Owen had been working and she had been lounging about, and although it was surprisingly tiring sitting still, she didn't mind. She enjoyed it.

"Yes?" She brought her attention back to him, which wasn't difficult. It was never difficult to look at Owen when he was working, with that little pinch between his brows and the intensity of his hazel eyes. He was a constant source of attraction for her, and that attraction was growing.

"You were wool gathering," he said, with a smile, watching her.

Wool gathering about *him*, she realized guiltily. She had been imagining herself reaching for him, winding her arms about his neck as he pressed himself against her on the red velvet chaise longue, his mouth covering hers and his hands on her body. She was rather overheated at the thought of it and wondered if he could somehow read her mind.

Ellis should be planning her future, thinking of ways in which she could travel to London and outwit Theo, and at the same time she should be in mourning for Archie and the life they had led. But it was all too painful. She just wanted to forget for a little while. Hide away at Hawthorne Lodge and pretend it had never happened. Was that wrong of her? If so, then she was very sorry, but she needed a moment to catch her breath. To just *be*.

Every morning when she rose, she looked forward to breakfast with Owen, and then a day of posing for him. At the end of the day they had dinner together, and the conversation was polite and comfortable—he did not ask her any difficult questions. She learned that his uncle had brought him up after his parents died, and he had no siblings. He had always aspired to be an artist, and he had found a niche where he was successful. "I never wanted to be beholden to my uncle for the clothes I wear and the food I eat. I am his heir, it's true, but I wanted to support myself as much as possible."

It occurred to Ellis that she had been beholden to Archie and had never given it a second thought. She imagined the expression on Archie's face if she had insisted on cooking her own dinner and making her own clothing and had to bite her lip on laughter. She had not thought of their marriage as one person being more significant than the other. She had helped Archie live the life he wanted, and he had saved her from her mother's ambitions.

But obviously Owen felt differently about his own personal arrangements. She wondered, a little worriedly, what he would think if he found out she was a duchess.

"What did you want me to do?" she asked now, meeting Owen's amused hazel eyes. There was a gentle warmth in them that seemed to feed the kernel of heat inside herself. Every time he looked at her that fire grew a little bigger, a little hotter.

"The story I'm telling needs to progress. We see the lady at ease, and then teasing her lover. Although the lover does not appear in the pictures, he is there. The people who buy the books can pretend *they* are the lady's lover. *They* are who she is gazing at so . . . wantonly." He cleared his throat. "At this stage I need to suggest that there has been some contact between them."

"Oh." She frowned. "But you will not include the lover in your pictures?"

"No. It is your expression, your manner, that will hint at the contact. Imagination plays a big part. Right now, I want you to look as if you have just been kissed," Owen said. "Messy and appealing. And wanting more."

By this time it was afternoon and the day was drawing to a close. Owen had spent most of the time sketching her face from different angles, and then her hands. He had even drawn her feet, which made her giggle. Nothing suggestive at all, which was disappointing.

This sounded much more exciting.

Ellis tried to imagine how a woman who had just been kissed would look, but she genuinely had no idea. "I've never been kissed," she blurted out. "At least, not in the way you are suggesting." Her cheeks heated and she knew they would be growing redder by the moment. He must think her a poor excuse for an artist's model.

His eyes had widened as he stared at her in amazement. "*Never?* But surely . . ." He bit his lip on what he had been about to say, however she could guess what he was thinking. Never been kissed? What sort of sheltered life had she lived? She supposed she should have pretended. And then she thought: Why couldn't this be her first kiss? Yes, technically, they were still mostly strangers, but she didn't feel like they were strangers. She felt as if she *knew* Owen. Certainly, she trusted him. Elijah had always said she would *know* when she met the right man.

Could that man be Owen?

"Do you think the lady in your book is someone like me, who has never been properly kissed?" she asked abruptly. "She could be on a journey, an . . . exploration of her senses. I am sure there are lots of single ladies who secretly long for such things while being obedient daughters or obliging sisters."

He stared and she could see he liked the idea. His hazel eyes seemed to shine green when he was excited by something. "That sounds . . . yes, Ellis, that is very good. An exploration of the senses." He pondered a moment and grinned. "I think my publisher would like that very much indeed."

Another idea came to her, a cunning idea, and she spoke before she could change her mind. "As this is my . . . *her* first kiss, I'm not exactly sure how I should look. Perhaps . . . maybe you should kiss me to make it more authentic?"

She could tell he was going to say no. If she had learned anything about Owen so far, it was that he prided himself on approaching his work in a strictly professional manner. He opened his mouth to speak but then stopped. "You want me to kiss you?" he repeated at last, as if he wanted to be sure he wasn't hearing things.

"Yes. If it will help with your drawing. You don't mind, do you? For the sake of your art?"

Was she laying it on too thick? Suddenly she had the horrible feeling he might not be interested in her in that way at all. She could have sworn he was, but perhaps he was just being kind. Or was it worse than that?

The words burst out of her. "I'm so sorry! Are you married or . . . or engaged? Is there someone else who—"

He held up his hand to stop her and she came to a halt.

She felt like such a fool! Just because the man drew salacious pictures did not mean he wasn't respectably married, probably with a brood of children with dark curls and eyes just like his.

"I am neither married nor engaged," he assured her, and there was amusement lurking in his eyes. He gave a cough to disguise a chuckle. "I have no paramour tucked away in the attic, either." And there was that hint of gentle teasing to make her heart flutter.

"No? Oh. Well, that's good then, isn't it? If I were your wife or—or fiancée, I would not want you kissing other women. In fact, I definitely would not."

She stopped, took a breath, and avoided his gaze.

"So, will you? Kiss me, I mean?"

When he hesitated, she was certain he would say no and talk about the need for integrity in their arrangement. But then he rose and came over to the chaise longue. She looked up at him, as he seated himself beside her.

He was going to do it. He was going to kiss her. He really was.

Owen reached out to cup her chin in his palm, and her lashes swept down, hiding her eyes, and her breathing quickened. She heard the rustle of his clothing as he moved closer, felt the warmth of his body, and then his lips pressed to hers, so lightly it felt barely more than the brush of a butterfly wing.

She trembled, she couldn't help it, and he went to draw back. But she didn't want him to stop, so she leaned in, and this time it was her lips that pressed to his.

He didn't pull back. He adjusted his hand, tilting her face a little, and his warm breath fanned her skin. The tip of his tongue ran along her bottom lip, and she gasped, and then his tongue dipped inside, deepening the kiss. She murmured, thoroughly enjoying the intimate experience. Blindly, needing to get closer, she reached up and slid her fingers through that wild mop of curls. His hair was soft, a little tangled, and she loved it. Her tongue touched his, tentatively at first, and then with a sense of desperation.

Oh, this was *nice*!

Their kiss deepened, grew more fervent. She even thought he might press her back onto the chaise longue. But he didn't. Slowly, delicately, his mouth lifted from hers, and his lips returned to the gentle press he had started with. One more soft kiss, and then he moved back.

She could not help it when her mouth followed his. Wanting more. She was struggling to breathe, and she knew her cheeks were flushed, heated with what could only be passion. Slowly she opened her eyes, lashes fluttering, and looked at him.

He was watching her avidly, and when he spoke his voice was raspy. "That's it. Stay exactly like that."

She tried not to be disappointed. She had to remind herself that he had only kissed her because she had wanted him to, and because he needed to capture the exact look he had spoken of. This had nothing to do with him desiring her.

She stilled her thoughts, watching as he picked up his sketchbook, his pencil flying over the paper as his eyes flicked back and forth to her. She wondered how she looked. Dazed, probably, and with her hair tumbling about her, and her eyes sleepy and her lips swollen, rather unhinged.

"Is this how you wanted me to look?" she whispered, barely moving her tingling lips.

"Exactly how," he murmured with satisfaction.

Chapter Nine

FOR A TIME after the kiss there was only the scratch of Owen's pencil to fill the silence between them. But as Ellis watched, he gradually became less frantic, sitting back to examine his work, and then changing a detail here and there. Ellis's lips still felt the ghost of their kiss.

"Owen," she began in a whisper. "Can I talk?"

"You can," he said, glancing up at her once more and then down at his work.

"You said you wanted to tantalize your audience. That this," she lifted a finger to gesture between them, "was about telling a story. A story about a lady who has never experienced a kiss or whatever comes next. But why has she chosen this man? *This* lover out of all the ones she could have chosen?"

He made another stroke, staring at the curve of her mouth. "I suppose at the heart of it, it is about a woman and a man, who are falling in—"

"Love?"

"Lust, more likely," he said, with a wicked grin that lodged in her chest and made her heart stutter. "He begins to seduce her, but she is his willing victim. In fact, it might be said she seduces him. That is up to the reader."

Ellis considered this. "And people will buy this book when it's finished?"

"I hope so. The others have sold well. Hugh Madrigal, my publisher has a select list of regular customers who buy everything I give him."

She considered that. "Do you think someone who knows me might buy your book and recognize me?"

He looked up then, meeting her eyes. "Does that concern you?" He frowned. "Of course it does. I should have thought. No. I would not let that happen. I can alter your face enough to hide your identity."

She nodded. She didn't really want him to do that. She wanted people to see *her* in his book, but what if Theo found out? It was a risk too great to take, although she told herself that by the time the book was published she would be safe in London. For a moment she considered what would happen if people bought the book and saw her in it. The shocked whispers, the stares . . . She would become notorious. The penniless girl who had married a duke, and now here she was, appearing in a saucy book.

She had expected Owen to ask her who might recognize her, but he didn't. He didn't pry, he was the complete gentleman—was it wrong of her to wish he weren't? She had to continually remind herself that they were two strangers who had come together for a brief time for the benefit of them both, and it was nothing more complicated than that.

Even if she might wish it were.

And yet that kiss . . . how could he not have felt it down to his very toes, just as she had?

He had set aside his sketch now and was smiling at her rather gravely. "Thank you, Ellis. That was perfect. I do not need you now. I can work on refining today's drawings by myself."

"Oh? Are we done?" She straightened, tucking her hair back behind her ears.

"Yes, until tomorrow. If you are happy to continue then?" He was watching her closely, as if he was worried the kiss might have changed her mind.

"Yes," she said softly. She rose to her feet, feeling a little lost. "Will I see you at dinner?"

"I . . . I may be working." He must have read her disappointment in her face because he added an explanation. "While everything is fresh in my mind."

It was embarrassing he had gauged her so easily. Ellis looked to the window. It was late afternoon, but this time of year it would remain light well into the evening. "I may go for a walk in your garden." She spoke with false enthusiasm.

"Please do. Don't stray too far," he said quickly. "Stay close to the house, and call out if . . ."

He was being protective, and she should be grateful, when all she wanted to do was keep on kissing him.

"I will," she reassured him firmly.

As she opened the door, she glanced back. He sat with his head bowed, busy sorting through today's work. He had already forgotten about her. She was just a means to an end, the latest in a long line of models, and she needed to remember that.

There was no one on the stairs as Ellis went up to her bed chamber. In the wardrobe were the gowns she had worn so far for Owen, but there were other garments, too. She decided several of them were unremarkable enough for her to wear outdoors. She chose one with a cream-colored skirt and a pale green bodice, with a matching ribbon to tie under her bosom. There were even some sturdy looking shoes which, if a little big, fit her well enough.

Once dressed, she examined herself in the mirror and thought she looked the epitome of respectability.

As promised, she would stay close by the house, but she did not believe Theo was still about. He would be at Breamore, putting his mark on everything and telling lies about her absence. She thought of Elijah and hoped he was still out of harm's way. After Archie had breathed his last, she had sent his lover to some relatives in a village nearby until it was safe for him to return. Although he had been no threat to Theo's plot, Ellis knew how much Theo had despised Archie and his paramour. He would wish to extract some sort of cruel revenge, she was sure, because that was just the sort of creature he was.

Theo's hatred seemed incomprehensible to Ellis, who had seen Archie and Elijah together and so obviously in love. Surely love was love, whoever it was between? She was only glad she had been able to give the two of them the chance to find happiness for a time at least.

Her thoughts wandered and she remembered one summer's evening, coming into the house barefoot after reading in the garden. The two men must not have heard her, because when she rounded the corner into the sitting room, they were together on the sofa. At first, she had thought they were cuddling, and then she saw that Elijah was lying on top of Archie, his hands clasping Archie's hips and lifting him so that he could push into him. They groaned together, and Elijah stretched down to kiss his lover, murmuring words that Ellis barely heard but knew were words of praise and love.

Unseen, she had slipped away and up to her room. The sight of them had not shocked her. She had known enough by then to understand the mechanics of men making love to each other. She had been happy for them, but at the same time she had been sad for herself. Because to see such affection, such devotion, between her two friends was to remind her that she was alone.

Outside, she took a turn about the garden. She could see over its sheltering wall, beyond the fields, to the forest. The trees looked as forbidding as she remembered, and with a shiver she turned her back. She was safe here at the Lodge. It was as if a warm cloak had been wrapped around her. As if Owen had enfolded her in his arms. Eventually she would have to leave, to begin the next stage of her life, but she didn't want to think about that now. She wanted to pretend she had no past and no future, and simply enjoy the attention Owen gave her every day.

Was it wrong of her to crave his single-minded attention? Surely that was rather childish. But there was more to Ellis's yearning than a selfish desire to be at the center of Owen's world. As the youngest of three daughters, she had often been ignored and overlooked. Catherine, the eldest, had been pushed into society by their mother and told to lead the way, and like the obedient girl she was, she had done just that. Ellis didn't believe for a moment that Catherine had wanted to marry her old duke, but still she had done it. He was dead now but had left her in a precarious position in the north of the country. Too far away to help Ellis in her current crisis.

Her second eldest sister, Sophia, had always been determined to make the most of her chances. She had once announced to them all that she would marry well—their mother didn't have to tell her to do so—and live a comfortable and busy life. She wanted to be at the center of London society, and make every other woman yearn to be her. So that was what she had done. Ellis did not like Sophia's husband. He was sly and secretive, and sometimes she thought Sophia wrapped herself in shawls and scarves for a reason. Did her husband hurt her? Not that Sophia would hear a word about that, shrugging and laughing, and turning the conversation to the next entertainment she was planning in her house in Mayfair. Ellis did not think she could ask Sophia for help. Her sister would be worried about the effect such a scandal would have on her position in the *ton*.

Ellis had felt alone, even when her sisters were with her. She remembered, when they were children, always trailing after them, calling for them to "please wait for me!" She had been so very grateful when Archie had found her and put his proposal to her and given her the chance to leave behind a life she loathed. It was just a shame her luck had not lasted, and she had found herself alone again. But during the past few days the clouds that seemed to hang over her had begun to clear away. Whether it was the effect of Owen, or Hawthorne Lodge, or both, she wasn't certain, but it was as if the sun was peeping out.

For a long time she remained in the garden, enjoying her solitude and the perfumed plants about her. The peacock strutted along the top of the wall, giving its distinctive screech. Joan had told her its name was Daffyd, and it had just appeared out of nowhere one morning. Privately, Ellis wondered if it was one of the peacocks Archie had brought to populate the gardens at Breamore. Perhaps, like her, it preferred the Lodge?

Eventually the light began to fade and a cool breeze wafted around her, stirring her hair and the lace on the sleeves of her gown. It was time to go inside. She hoped Owen would be at dinner, but she already knew he would not. He wanted to finish his work, and she understood that. She had noticed he was a bit of a perfectionist when it came to his art.

She smiled. And he had kissed her! The warm pressure of his lips had been quite delightful, and then the slide of his tongue. She had been certain he was going to keep kissing her, but he had stopped. It had all been about his desire to ensure her look, her pose, was just as he wanted it, and not his desire for her as a person.

Such a lowering thought.

But what about tomorrow? If his series of drawings was about seduction, then what came after a kiss? She shivered a little, hugging herself. A touch? Would she actually have to pretend she had just been made love to?

Suddenly she knew she didn't want to pretend.

Ellis trailed her fingers over some climbing roses that grew against the wall of the house. The petals were soft and fragrant. Could she persuade Owen to make love to her? She imagined him nuzzling against her throat, his tongue warm and wet as he slid it down to her breasts, his mouth hot as he sucked on her nipples. They began to ache, as if imagination were fact. This was desire. If only she were more experienced with real life than the fiction in her books, she could . . .

Could what? *Seduce* him? Like the lady in his series of drawings? And then what would happen? Would he finish his work and be finished with her? Send her off to London and forget all about her?

It came to her as no shock, but Ellis didn't want that. She didn't want him to forget her. She wanted her time here to go on and on, for it never to end. She wanted him to kiss her again and hold her. She wanted him to ask her to stay with him forever.

So foolish.

She knew better. The thought sobered her, and she quickened her steps, making her way back to the door and into the house.

Chapter Ten

HE SHOULDN'T HAVE kissed her. Owen groaned and tunnelled his hands into his hair, giving it a hard tug that hurt. He had broken his first rule when it came to his sitters. He had allowed himself to feel, to think of her as a woman, instead of viewing her as a means to an end.

The warmth of her lips, the sweet puff of her breath, and the utter wonder of that kiss they had shared . . .

The result had been a brilliant sketch, and he only hoped he had fully captured the dazed look in her eyes and the flush in her cheeks. Just thinking about it made his cock harden, and he wasn't sure what to do about it. Over the past few days, being with her, cataloguing every part of her, had only increased his attraction for Ellis.

It was starting to feel like an obsession.

And yet at the same time, Owen was doing some of his best work. He knew it, and he knew Hugh Madrigal would recognize it, too. Owen could just imagine his publisher's excitement when presented with this new series. Hugh was always enthusiastic, but this time he'd be incandescent! In such circumstances, how could Owen walk away from Ellis?

One thing he *could* do was distance himself a little. Not seeing her again until the morning had felt like a good idea, even though the disappointment in her face when he said he did not think he would be at dinner had nearly made him change his mind. But he hadn't, and an evening apart might mean he could regain some of the equilibrium he had lost.

The troubling thing was, Ellis was attracted to him, too. He had seen it in her face, the tentative smile, the way she gazed at him with her big brown eyes. Owen knew this sometimes happened—it had even happened to him. Models thought themselves in love with the artist. The close attention they experienced tricked them into believing it was more than just a brief, professional relationship. There were many stories throughout history to illustrate this, and he knew of artists who were more than happy to bed their models, arguing it was a perquisite of the job.

But Owen had always sworn he would not take advantage. Even if he was tempted, he refused to act upon that temptation.

Until now.

He groaned again and gave his hair another hard tug. That seemed to do the trick, and he took a deep breath and steadied himself, before looking down at the drawings spread before him. They really were the best he'd ever done. Kissing her had meant the outcome on paper was even better than he could have imagined. The question was, could he walk that fine line between professional and cad, until he was finished with the series? Could he then smile at her and send her on her way to London?

He wasn't sure that he could. He didn't even know if what she had told him about her escape in the forest was the truth, but he suspected not. After Joan had informed him about the coach, she had sent some of the servants to investigate Ellis's story.

Only there had been nothing to find. No sign of a coach, and no sign of the pistol-wielding highwaymen.

Whatever had sent Ellis running for her life was gone. If it had ever existed. Did that mean she had lied? Owen had seen for himself the angry gentleman who had come to the door of the lodge and demanded to know if she was inside. There must be some truth in it.

Joan had tut-tutted at Owen when he had admitted he was reluctant to delve into Ellis's private business.

"Sometimes there is being *too* much of a gentleman," she had scolded. "Let us hope these angry men do not return before you finish your drawings."

Owen knew that sometimes he was a selfish being, more focused on his art than the world around him, and he preferred not to interfere in matters that might take his attention away from his endeavors.

Maybe it was time he changed that.

His uncle had always indulged him. The elderly confirmed bachelor had a fondness for his nephew, and Owen would be forever grateful for his kindness in taking in a small boy he hardly knew. Owen was certain it must have been a great shock to the viscount to find himself the sole protector of a child who cried in the night for his parents and refused to eat and spent most of his time scribbling on paper.

Uncle Steven often teased Owen and exclaimed in disgust over some of his work, but Owen knew that if it came down to it, the viscount would protect his nephew's right to do as he wished to his last breath.

Owen could have lived with his uncle in London, and he had for a time, but he did not enjoy the hustle and bustle of life in the capital. He was not a social creature by nature, and when the canvases and sketchbooks began to pile up in Owen's bedchamber and creep into the rest of the house, his uncle had suggested his nephew might be better off in the country. "Hawthorne Lodge is just the place. No one for miles to bother you. And if the neighbors invite you to a soiree you can lock the doors and refuse to go. Take Joan with you," he'd declared magnanimously. "She's just as averse to company as you."

And that was how Owen had come to the Lodge, and he'd never left.

There had been no pressure for him to marry, despite being

eight and twenty years now. And anyway, his uncle was hardly one to talk of matrimony when he had never shown the slightest interest in that institution himself. Owen had indulged himself with women over the years, but it had never turned into anything serious. He had always drifted away when his physical interest waned, or perhaps it was the women who drifted away. Despite being a lord, he didn't think he was much of a catch. What wife would want to spend her time at Hawthorne Lodge twiddling her thumbs when she could be in London going to balls and visiting her friends?

Although he wasn't inexperienced when it came to ladies, he still wasn't at all sure what this feeling for Ellis was. Yes, he was attracted to her physically, but it felt different . . . deeper, and far less civilised than anything he had ever experienced before. Shockingly, when he was with her, Owen sometimes felt as if he might lose his much-lauded gentlemanly restraint entirely.

His thoughts were so muddled, he was relieved when Polly knocked on the door and carried in a tray.

Was it time to eat? When he became too wrapped up in his work and in his head, the two women scolded him as if he were still five years old.

"Tea and cake." Polly set the tray down. She glanced at his desk, and then, when her curious gaze latched onto the sketch on top, she went still. "Oh!" she said softly. "That is very striking, my lord." Her eyes narrowed and she tilted her head to see better. It was the drawing of Ellis, hair loose about her, clothing rumpled, and looking "well-kissed."

"Miss Mallory is a very good at striking a pose," he said stiffly. "She has inspired me."

"I can see that," Polly murmured, with a lift of her eyebrows. "Forgive me, but she looks almost as if she has been kissing someone. Kissing them all afternoon." Her gaze slid slyly to Owen.

"As I said, she is very good." Owen was aware he sounded defensive. "Now, if you don't mind, I am very busy."

Polly nodded but lingered, ignoring his hint. "You know that Joan hopes . . ." The words drifted off.

Owen waited but she seemed disinclined to speak again, still staring down at the image of Ellis. He could let it go. It was probably better if he did. But he was irritated and anxious, and suddenly he wanted to know what it was his housekeeper hoped for when it came to him.

"What do you think Joan hopes?" he asked lightly.

Just as Polly said, "Did you like the outfit Miss Mallory wore today?"

"It was superb," Owen admitted.

Ellis had appeared at breakfast in a white sheath with a belt at her waist and sandals wrapped about her calves. She looked like a Roman slave, or a goddess. He vaguely remembered having the outfit made for a series of drawings a year or so ago, but the project had fallen through, and it had never been used.

Polly's eyes lit up. "It was, wasn't it? Miss Mallory is a beautiful woman. And," she tapped her finger against the sketch, "I think she is smitten with you."

Owen had been thinking the same thing, but now he denied it. "Of course she isn't. We barely know each other. Is that what Joan hopes for, for me and Miss Mallory to fall in love and marry and live happily ever after? I can't see it, I'm sorry, Polly. Now, if you don't mind . . ."

"But are you happy now?" Polly asked, obviously not going anywhere. She was like that when she got a bee in her bonnet. "I know that you have me and Joan—and who could deny we are great company—but aren't you sometimes lonely, my lord? You should not let what happened with Merrily make you unable to trust."

He sighed. "Polly, I have never enjoyed the society of others. Occasionally, yes, but mostly, no. And as for Merrily . . . I'm well rid of her."

"Doesn't everyone need someone to talk to when they feel sad or lonely? Someone to cuddle up to in bed." Polly must have seen something in his eyes and winced. "Sorry, have I gone too far, sir? I should know your boundaries by now, but I worry. And I know Joan does, too."

Owen cleared his throat. "You have definitely gone too far, Polly." Then, curious despite himself, "Do I *need* someone to cuddle up to in bed? I go to bed to sleep, not to cuddle."

She answered tartly. "Well, Joan said she heard you pacing last night, as if you couldn't sleep. Besides, everyone needs a cuddle now and again. If you want my opinion, there's not much point to having a life if you can't share it with someone special." Polly finished with a respectful curtsy she clearly didn't mean and left him to his solitude.

Owen stared after her, and wondered if he should give her notice. For a moment he imagined the satisfaction it would give him . . . until she started to cry and Joan began to shout. No, he knew he wouldn't do it. He was too fond of Joan and Polly, and they of him, and he knew how precarious their lives together were. He would do everything he could to protect them.

His thoughts strayed to Polly's words despite himself. Had Joan really heard him pacing last night? He seemed to be pacing most nights, his emotions unsettled and confused. He suspected it was because he wanted things he couldn't have, his baser instincts battling with his chivalrous ones. Ellis Mallory seemed to have turned his heart and mind into a battleground. Not to mention his sexual desire for her. *That* was raging.

This afternoon when she had asked him to kiss her . . . in God's name, had the woman no sense of self-preservation? For all she knew he could be a ravening beast and here she was, asking him to gobble her up! Owen gave a brief bark of laughter, only to groan again in the next moment.

He needed to get through the rest of the series of drawings, to finish *The Lady's Sensual Journey* or whatever he was going to call it, so that he could send it on to Hugh, and bundle Ellis off to London. That was all he had to do. The trouble was that the next drawings in the series would be the most daring, the most sensual. The lady at rest was all very well, but now the lady had been kissed and soon she would be touched and then, God help him, her body would be taken, consumed, and the passion and pleasure would grow and grow, until—

Abruptly Owen stood up, wincing at the obvious and painful bulge in his breeches.

Perhaps it would help if he sought out a woman in the village? There must be someone? The trouble was he had never had the need to pay for tupping. The women in London had been practiced and sophisticated. Willing to come to bed with him, while at the same time they had been aware that it was nothing more than a momentary pleasure.

Despite her secrets, he already knew Ellis was neither sophisticated nor practiced.

Movement caught his eye beyond the window, and when he stepped closer, he saw that Ellis was standing in the walled garden with her arms clasped about herself. She was wearing something quite different from the outfits she had donned for her sittings with him. It didn't matter, she could be in sackcloth, and he would think her exquisite.

She moved then, as if to return to the house, and he saw her expression more clearly. Bereft, as if the weight of the world was upon her shoulders.

What was she thinking? Was it about what happened to her in the forest that day? What were her secrets? Because he instinctively knew there was more than one.

Ellis had passed by the window and out of sight, but Owen remained staring out. The day was fading, and he reminded himself he had much to do. But as he went to turn away something else caught his eye. A reflection, a brief flash of silver, coming from the edge of the forest.

Was someone there? What could have caused such a thing? A horse's bridle, or a buckle or an ornament, catching the last of the sunlight?

He stood and watched, but whatever he had seen did not

come again. By then he had decided it was nothing important after all and, pushing aside all thoughts of Ellis, Owen went back to his work.

Chapter Eleven

THE NEXT MORNING when Ellis came down to breakfast, she learned that Owen had gone away to the nearest large town for the day. Joan said he had to collect some art supplies that had been sent from London, and he wouldn't be back until late. If then.

"Sometimes he stays over for a day or two," Joan said.

Ellis was disappointed, and she wondered if this was her fault. Was he intentionally avoiding her after their kiss? He hadn't come to dinner the night before, and it had been a quiet affair on her own. She was used to her own company at Breamore, although Archie and Elijah were always there if she needed them. But she still spent a great deal of time alone.

It felt different now because she had begun to enjoy being with Owen, looked forward to it. She was becoming reliant upon him, and she wasn't completely sure if that was a good thing. Recently she had learned how her world could change in an instant, and there was only herself she could really trust. Yes, he had helped her escape a potentially tragic situation, but did that mean she should look upon him as someone who had her best interests at heart? Why did she feel as if she *knew* him?

After breakfast she did some exploring. The Lodge was not a big house. With thick stone walls and small windows—apart from the one in Owen's study—it was built as a shelter from the dangers outside. Which made it seem appropriate that she was here, taking sanctuary.

She found some shelves of books in a sitting room and spent some time browsing them but there was nothing that took her interest, apart from one of Owen's picture books. She took the book up to her room and looked through it from cover to cover, agog at the beauty of his drawings while at the same time imagining herself in those poses.

As she examined the images, she realized she felt a little envious. Owen had sat with these women, he had seen every curve of their bodies, every expression on their faces. In a way, he had known them intimately. And that was when she admitted she didn't want him to draw anyone but her.

"You are being ridiculous," she told herself.

But she couldn't seem to help it. From the moment Owen had first opened the door to her, she had been captivated by him in a way she had never been by any man before. What on earth was she going to do about it?

In an attempt to escape her own thoughts, she set aside the book and returned downstairs. When she heard voices coming from the dining room, she wondered if Owen was back. Her heart began to beat faster and her lips tingled, as if preparing for another kiss, and she hurried forward. When she found the door ajar, she peeped around it.

There was no sign of Owen. Joan and Polly were sitting together in one of the chairs by the window, or rather, Joan was sitting in the chair and Polly was sitting on her lap. For a moment Ellis wasn't sure what she was seeing, and then Polly wound her arms around the housekeeper's neck and kissed her. Joan did not struggle or push her away. She kissed her back.

Ellis made a sound. Immediately afterward she jumped out of sight, a hand covering her mouth. She hoped the two women had not heard her. Surely, they were too engrossed in each other? Until now she had not guessed that Joan and Polly were lovers, although remembering back to some of the smiles and the glances they had exchanged, she supposed she should have suspected.

The door was flung fully open and she gasped.

Joan stood there with Polly peeping over her shoulder. "Miss Mallory," the housekeeper said. There was a silence, and no one seemed prepared to fill it.

"I'm sorry," Ellis said. "I thought I heard voices and wondered if Owen—Lord Lyndhurst—had returned home."

"And instead you found us," Joan replied sternly. "If you are thinking of informing his lordship about Polly and myself then you are wasting your time."

Ellis's eyes widened in distress. "Oh no, I wouldn't do that. And besides, I'm sure he knows already, doesn't he? He is very fond of you both. And there's no reason why you shouldn't love each other. I . . . I had two friends, gentlemen, who were lovers."

Polly and Joan exchanged one of their glances, and Polly smiled.

"It was just . . ." Ellis went on, her words tumbling out. "I am beginning to wonder if everyone in the world has someone to love apart from me."

"Aw, there's someone, I'm sure," said kind-hearted Polly. "I was talking to his lordship just the other day and—" She stopped when Joan shot her a warning glance.

"I think you are being disingenuous," Joan said. "You look like the sort of woman who is usually surrounded by a throng of admirers."

Ellis gave a shaky laugh. "Sadly, no. But then again, I do not want to be pursued for . . ." For her wealth, she was going to say, but thought better of it. "I want that one man who will love me for myself, and who I will love back. For better or worse, I am a romantic."

Polly sighed, while Joan gave her an irritated look. "And you believe that man is Lord Lyndhurst? He is not someone to act against his principles. He has always had a moral code when it comes to his sitters, but Merrily, the last woman he employed to sit for him, shattered his trust and—"

"And now he finds it impossible to set aside his honorable nature in case I am another Merrily," Ellis finished for her.

"Exactly." Joan hesitated, and added, "That's not to say you can't persuade him to go against his principles if you try hard enough. Although I'm not sure he will thank you for it afterward. Especially if you have some secret you haven't told him and which he will not like."

Ellis knew her face was on fire. "Thank you. I have my own reasons for not . . . that is . . ." She stumbled to a close and took a step back. "I'm sorry I interrupted. Please, be assured, I wish you only happiness." And she turned and walked away.

Her muddled thoughts began to clear. She was attracted to Owen. She had enjoyed the feel of his lips on hers, the taste of him, the closeness. Last night she had been restless and aching, as if her senses, once awakened, could not be subdued. Daringly, she had run her hands over her breasts, imagining it was Owen touching her, and when the tingle ignited between her thighs, she had pressed her fingers there and wondered what it would be like if Owen made love to her.

She wanted *that*, she wanted *him*.

Now that Ellis knew more about Merrily, she suspected she was the reason Owen was so wary around her. Because of Merrily he would refuse to do any of the things she longed for him to do. If it was up to him and his "moral code," he would wave goodbye to her as soon as he had finished his series of drawings. But Ellis wanted Owen to show her the pleasures to be had with a man she admired and desired. She wasn't a fool. He may not be her Elijah, or her Polly, and what she was feeling may not be everlasting love, but there was a strong attraction between them. A sense that despite their short acquaintance she already knew him. She felt it, and she believed Owen could feel it too.

It would be such a waste to ignore it.

Ellis had never seduced anyone in her life, but surely it wasn't that difficult? She had wanted him to kiss her, and he had. If she didn't try, if she let this opportunity pass her by, then she knew she would regret it for the rest of her days. And if Theo had anything to do with it, those days may not be many.

Joan had warned her that even though she may be able to win Owen over, he might not appreciate it afterward. That was a risk, but it was one she was willing to take.

❖

Chapter Twelve

THE NEXT MORNING Polly arrived to help her dress in the turquoise satin—the mermaid dress, as Ellis had named it. Until then she had wondered if Owen was still away, but the maid informed her that he had returned last night and was eager to begin work again.

Owen had already breakfasted and left the room by the time Ellis arrived, and she made haste to finish a slice of toast and drink her tea after an unsmiling Joan had informed her, "He's waiting in his study for you, Miss Mallory."

Ellis had almost forgotten her intrusion into the housekeeper's love life, but Joan obviously hadn't.

The door to the study was open, and Owen was seated at his desk. His dark hair was as untidy as ever, several curls dangling over his forehead as he leaned into his work. Her heart began to beat faster, and she took a breath. She imagined herself sitting on his lap, like Polly and Joan, and winding her arms around his neck. She imagined the laughter in his eyes and the welcoming kisses he would give her.

Impulsively she took a step forward, and her dress rustled.

Owen looked up.

Just for a moment she thought she saw naked joy in his face before his expression shuttered. His hazel eyes, so warm when he had first looked at her, were wary now, and there were shadows under them. Hope sank like a leaky boat. It seemed she had been right about him regretting the kiss and now he was determined to hold himself at a distance, determined to be a principled gentleman. Why couldn't he be a scoundrel? But Ellis knew if he had been a scoundrel then she wouldn't have wanted to throw herself into his arms.

"We have a busy day ahead of us," he said in a brisk, business-like voice. "I need to finish the final sketches and send them to my publisher as soon as possible. He is growing impatient."

He smiled as he said it, but Ellis felt the gap widen between them. "Of course," she said, hiding her disappointment. "Should I undress . . .?"

He swallowed and looked away, avoiding her gaze. "Ah, no. Not yet. I need some more drawings of your hands and your . . . your feet."

Ellis wanted to laugh. Instead, she sat primly on the chaise longue and removed her slippers. She was wearing stockings today, and it occurred to her that she could remove them in a slow and seductive manner to see how he reacted.

If he really wasn't interested in her he would be impatient, wanting to get on with his work. But Ellis didn't think that was going to happen.

She stood and put one foot on the chaise longue and drew her skirt up over her knee. Slowly she undid the tie, and slid the stocking down over her knee, over her calf, and over her foot. She wriggled her toes.

Ellis looked at him through her lashes.

He was unmoving, gazing at her with rapt attention, so she lifted her other foot and began to remove that stocking too.

"Stay like that." His voice startled her.

"Like this?" Her stocking was about her ankle, the shape of her lower leg exposed as she leaned forward. She gave him a sideways glance.

"Yes."

He was already working feverishly, as if he must get the image down while it was fresh in his mind. *Before he sent her away.* That thought made her sad, because if it were up to Ellis, then she would never leave.

Last night, as she had looked through his book again, she had made a plan. But this morning when she walked into his room, she hadn't been at all certain she would go through with it. Now, seeing his reaction to her, *feeling* her reaction to him, she knew she had to try.

"I've been thinking about your series," she said, aiming to sound as if her heart wasn't beating so anxiously.

He stopped and gave her a curious look, but his eyes were still guarded. "About my series?"

Well, now it was too late to change her mind, and she could not stop even if she wanted to. "Yes."

The silence drew out and his mouth twitched into a smile. "Tell me then?"

This seduction thing was not as easy as she'd hoped. Ellis continued, hoping she didn't sound panicky. "I read a great deal. Mainly romances. What you are doing now . . . this series . . . it seems like a romance to me, only with pictures instead of words."

"That's fair," he agreed cautiously. Before adding with a wry grin, "Perhaps a rather saucy romance."

She laughed in relief. "Yes. One of the more risqué romances that some people want prohibited from sale."

He nodded at that and waited. She took another breath and reminded herself she had nothing to lose. Either he agreed with her idea, or he said no and they carried on as they were until she left for London.

"I wondered if . . . could *I* suggest a pose? Something that would appeal to me if I was a reader." She hurried on when he didn't interrupt. "You said your patrons included ladies as well as gentlemen?"

"There are definitely ladies interested in my work," he agreed. "In fact, rather a lot of them. I've often wondered what the appeal is."

"I wonder if they are married ladies, or single women of means?" Ellis pondered. "Do they look at your pictures and dream of themselves in the place of your models? Maybe they spin a story in their imaginations to fit the images? Are they unhappily married or do they long to spice up a tired relationship? Or are they simply lonely?"

Like Ellis.

She hadn't meant to say so much, but Owen seemed to be watching her with amused interest. She felt her cheeks heat.

"You've obviously given it a great deal of thought," he said. "I like to think they are art lovers who admire the quality of my work."

"There is that possibility," she said, with a smile.

"You were going to tell me about your idea," he reminded her gently. "The pose?"

"Can I show you instead?"

"Of course." He had left his desk for the chair opposite the chaise longue, and now he sat down. "You know you don't have to do anything you don't want to, Ellis."

Why did he have to be so good, so earnest? Blast Merrily for making him so cautious when Ellis needed him to be rash and irresponsible. But, she reminded herself, only with her and no one else. She met his eyes, and noticed there was a spark in them, a little hint that what came out of his mouth may not be what was in his head, and it gave her the courage to carry on.

"It is all a fairy story, is it not? We are indulging your readers, leading them one step at a time, toward a—a climax."

He looked down at the word, but he was smiling. "Go on."

She reached back to undo her dress, pretending that she couldn't quite reach. "Do you mind?" she asked him, turning so that her back was to him.

She heard Owen clear his throat, and then his fingers were dealing with her hooks and buttons. If she was not mistaken, they trembled slightly.

"How many do you want undone?" he asked, and his breath brushed against her nape. She felt goosebumps. He was so close, and the combination of his warm body and the citrus scent of his pomade made her almost dizzy.

"All of them," she said.

His fingers hesitated, and she held her breath, waiting. But then he resumed, a little clumsily, until he said, "That's all of them," and moved back.

Ellis readied herself. She pictured Owen standing before her, watching her, but instead of trying to resist her, he was urging her on. Of course, Owen didn't need to know she was thinking that. Any hint that she was trying to seduce him, and he would walk out and close the door behind him.

"I am imagining I am one of your female patrons," she said, and held her hand against the bodice. If she took it away, her gown would fall to her waist, and she wasn't ready to go that far. Not yet. "I think if I were, I would not want my lover to undress me. I would want to undress *for* him. Display myself for his—his pleasure."

Her face must be on fire. She did not look at him as she lay down on the chaise longue and drew the hem of the gown up to her knees, and then rested her head against the cushion at the end. Her hair was near enough to loose, tumbling about her. She wriggled, allowing her bodice to slip low over the globes of her breasts.

Was that far enough? Daringly, she allowed the bodice to slip again, until one pink nipple was exposed.

She heard Owen's breath catch. A glance at him told Ellis he was most definitely engaged. Seeing his throat moving as he swallowed made her want to smile but she knew he could still change his mind. Please don't let him start talking about professional and gentlemanly behavior!

"Is this too much?" she said in a whisper, not wanting to break the spell.

"No, it's perfect," he said, his voice also hardly more than a whisper. "I'll just . . ." He began to draw, she could hear the sound of his pencil on the paper, and the creak of his chair as he shifted about on it.

As Ellis lay there, half naked before him, any embarrassment or doubt began to diminish. She felt surprisingly free. It was as if she had cast off her former life and become someone else. Would people look at her in Owen's book and want to be her? Would they pretend they were in her place and make up a story to dream about? She hoped so, because she was making up her own story right now. A romance about her and Owen.

She brushed her fingers over her nipple and felt it tighten and ache. An answering ache joined in from between her thighs, and she gave a gasp because it felt so good, and then did it again.

"You . . . are you . . ." Owen began, his voice shaky. And then a gruff, "Never mind. Don't move. That's perfect."

Ellis tried not to smile. "You say that a great deal. *Perfect.* I know I am not the only woman who has posed for you."

"No," he glanced at her quickly. "There have been others. But no one like . . . you are . . ." He chewed on his lip, bent his head so that a dark and glossy curl fell over his forehead.

"I am what?" she asked, her curiosity stronger than her fear of what he might say.

"You're not like any of them," he said, and looking up met her eyes with that bright hazel stare.

Surely that was a compliment. "I'm a conundrum," she replied.

He gave an abrupt laugh. "You could say that *cariad.*" His gaze sharpened, the green in his eyes suddenly more prominent. "I wish I knew what you were, Ellis."

Was he asking her to tell him? She opened her mouth and closed it again. She couldn't, not yet, not now. If she told him the truth, he would immediately revert into the honorable gentleman, and her chance to seduce him would be gone.

Chapter Thirteen

OWEN WATCHED HER, trying to read her mind, but she seemed determined to keep her own council. His heart sank. Whatever the truth was, she did not trust him enough to share it with him. He had known she had been lying from the start, but he hadn't pressed her. It hadn't been in his selfish interests to do so. But now he did care, and that she wouldn't tell him hurt more than he had expected.

He reminded himself how Merrily had lied to him, stolen his money and his work, and gone off to London. How he had sworn he would not let himself be taken in again, and now here he was.

It was all very well to tell himself that she was no more than a stranger who had come into his life, briefly, and would soon be gone again. The truth was he had been attracted to her from the first moment. Instantaneous connection. Love—or was it lust?— at first sight. He might struggle, but every day he spent in her company only pulled him deeper into this emotional morass.

"Let us get on," he said in a purposelessly detached voice. "You've moved. Lie back the way you were a moment ago."

She did as he asked, attempting to relax, watching him cautiously, as if at any moment he might begin shouting at her. Owen had known this would be difficult. The most beautiful woman he had ever seen was spread before him like a feast and although he was starving, he could not indulge. She had been a little self-conscious earlier, when she suggested the pose, but had seemed to throw aside her doubts.

His pencil stilled. Was she teasing him? His eyes followed the hypnotic movement of her finger on her pink nipple. Was she trying to lure him into behaving in a way he had sworn he would not?

He had already kissed her, and now he *ached* for her. He had hoped his time away might have calmed his passion for her, and he had thought at first it had, but here it was roaring back to life again, only twice as bad. He couldn't sleep at night for thinking about her, and his days were filled with being in close contact with the one thing he denied himself. He wasn't sure how long he could hold out. He didn't even know if he wanted to!

Ellis gave a little shiver.

It was his opportunity to turn away, hurrying to stoke the coals in the fireplace back to life. He took his time about it, kneeling on the hearth, until he had his body under control again. When he turned back, she was watching him with a little frown between her brows. She had drawn up the bodice to her throat and was clutching it there like some sort of maiden under threat.

"I didn't realize how cold the room had become," he explained, trying for a smile. "Is that better?"

She nodded, her hair falling about her, and then her eyes widened. "Oh! I have moved again."

"Never mind. Let me . . ." He stepped forward to arrange her back into the pose, and only realized his mistake when it was too late.

As he reached for the turquoise cloth, to slip it back down over her breast, his fingers touched her skin. At the same time, Ellis reached for the same piece of cloth, and their fingers fumbled, tangled. She pulled her hand back and her bodice fell away and there she was. Naked to the waist. Desire raged through him as hot as wildfire. Unstoppable. Incinerating all his resolutions in its path.

He groaned. The sound came out of him before he could stop it. She leaned toward him, winding her arms about his neck and drawing him close. He didn't struggle, he came willingly. It was impossible to do anything else.

Her mouth was as warm and willing as he remembered. He tilted his head for better access, his tongue slipping inside. Heaven. Good sense tried to shout to him, but it was drowned out by desire and need, and an urgency he could not remember ever feeling in his life before.

Either she pulled him down or he tumbled over, because now he was lying on top of her, still fully clothed. He was no longer resisting. Whatever had held him back before was forgotten, and he groaned again as he explored her mouth. Her lips were so soft and willing, and she was so addictive. He wanted more.

Owen lifted his weight off her with one arm, his other hand cupping the lush mound of her breast. Her nipple prodded into his palm, and he bent and took it into his mouth. She arched up with a soft cry, and he used his tongue to caress her, rolling the nub and then sucking hard.

"Oh, you . . . that . . . oh!" She gasped, sensible words seemingly beyond her.

His desire was raging now, but finally good judgment began to make itself heard. He should turn back. He should get to his feet right now and move away.

As if she was aware he was on a knife edge, she said, "Please," and when he looked down into her brown eyes, they were full of want, of need. "Please make love to me," she breathed against his lips and reached up to kiss him again.

She was giving him permission, and Owen slipped over the precipice.

Her skirt was already rucked up to her thighs, and he slid his hand over her soft skin, finding nothing to stop him when his hand cupped her mound. Her breath stuttered, and he could feel how wet she was, how ready. His fingers brushed against her opening, testing her response.

Ellis gave a little moan, pushing toward him, her thighs falling open. Owen wanted to lie between them, to push his long-suffering cock inside her, and that was when he remembered he was still fully dressed. Dazed, he sat up, reaching for buttons and ties, shrugging off his jacket and pulling his shirt over his head and throwing it carelessly aside. Ellis rested back on her elbows, watching him with wanton eyes. She reached out her hand, and he felt the warm slide of her fingers over the hair on his chest, following it down to his stomach, where the dark trail vanished beneath his breeches.

He went to unbutton the flap but then paused, his gaze meeting hers. As much as he wanted to rut against her like an animal, his gentlemanly instincts were ingrained. "Are you sure?"

She gave a choked little laugh. "Very sure. Don't stop."

With a hard grin, he undid the buttons and his cock pushed aside the flap of cloth that was covering it, so eager he almost laughed. Her eyes widened, but she wasn't daunted. A moment later she was stroking his hard, aching flesh, and this time Owen groaned so loudly he was afraid everyone in the house could hear him.

She wrapped her fingers around him as best she could, but Owen was sure that if she kept touching him, then he would spill. And that wasn't what he wanted. He wanted to be inside her. He wanted to make her his in the most fundamental, and possibly ungentlemanly, of ways.

He shuffled down the chaise longue, until his panting breath was against her thigh, and then he leaned in and breathed her in. Warm and delicious. He parted her soft flesh with his tongue and found her soaked. She arched up against him and then her hands tangled in his hair, holding him against her.

"Oh God . . . oh Owen," she managed in a strangled voice.

He licked again, and then sucked on that hard bundle of nerves that made her thigh muscles shake and her hands tighten painfully in his hair. She was on the verge of coming and suddenly he wanted that. He wanted to bring her to her peak. His own pleasure was important, but hers was more so. Bringing her to her climax felt like a matter of pride to him.

She was so close. As he licked and sucked, her hands tightened more and more, her body arching against his mouth like a bow. He was playing her like an instrument, and she was about to reach her crescendo.

With a gasping cry she went rigid beneath him, until she fell back, boneless and replete. Her chest rose and fell, drawing in short breaths that slowly lengthened.

Owen sat up, wiping his mouth with his hand, and gazed down at her. He felt as if he was the most powerful man in the world. He wasn't sure whether or not that was a good thing, but he couldn't help it. He was the king of all men, as he looked down at her flushed cheeks and her dazed eyes. He had done this. He had made her look like this.

After a moment he noticed that although she was still wearing the dress, it was rucked up about her waist, so she was essentially naked. There was something of great abandon about that, and he itched to record it on paper, but for once he resisted his creative desires in favor of his physical ones.

He closed his hand over his cock, stroking himself. In a moment he would be pushing inside her, deep, into that moist warmth. He leaned forward, nuzzling against her throat, the tip of his shaft entering her that first little bit.

"May I?" he asked politely and felt her shake with laughter.

"Oh, you may, indeed you may . . ." she began.

Just as there was a sharp knock on the door.

It took Owen a moment to become aware of Joan's voice on the other side because of his blood roaring in his ears. Another moment for him to comprehend what she was saying.

"My Lord? There is a man here asking to see Miss Mallory. Sir? He says his name is Elijah Jones."

Owen was looking down at Ellis and he saw her eyes widen. She blinked, and suddenly the dazed, sated look vanished. She started to rise and when his weight prevented her, she pushed at him. Owen stumbled from the chaise longue, still dizzy with desire, still aching. She refused to look at him as she tugged up her gown, or perhaps she had forgotten him altogether. She smoothed down the skirt and then began to fasten the back.

He noticed that she was perfectly capable of doing it herself, and the last of his desire slipped away.

"Who is Elijah?" he asked sharply.

"Someone I . . ." She hesitated and took a breath. Her eyes avoided his. "He is important to me, and I must speak to him."

Important to her? He watched as she went to the door, but it was only when she glanced back, raising her eyebrows as her eyes slid up and down him, that he remembered he was still half naked, his chest bare and his softening cock exposed. Self-conscious, Owen turned his back and began hastily to put himself to rights.

She opened the door just as he retrieved his sketchbook and pretended to examine it. He didn't want to meet Joan's gaze—she would know what had been happening in here. He wasn't sure if he was ashamed. Disappointed in himself, yes. Confused, yes. But the chief feeling was a growing distrust when it came to Ellis.

He heard her ask where Elijah was, and Joan's reply that he was outside in the garden. She hurried away, her satin dress rustling eagerly, and the front door opened and closed. He hoped Joan had gone too, but then she spoke.

"Well," she said softly.

"Not now," he barked. "Really, Joan, not now."

He was grateful that for once she took him at his word. When her steps had carried her away, Owen closed his eyes and wondered what on earth he thought he was doing. Had he really broken all his rules, and for a woman who would not even tell him what she was doing here? Did he never learn?

He had tunnelled his hands into his hair, about to give a hard tug, when he realized he could see Ellis outside his window. There she was, standing in the walled garden, a vision among the flowers. She was calling out for this Elijah, and then a stranger appeared behind her, and rested his hand on her shoulder.

Ellis turned to him and the expression on her face . . . it was an agonizing mixture of pain and joy. And then Elijah clasped her in his arms and Owen felt his own hands clench at his sides. He wasn't sure what emotion was swirling around inside him as he watched them, but it was something dark and dangerous. The sort of feeling he would never have thought himself capable of.

Until now.

Chapter Fourteen

ELLIS HURRIED OUT of the door, only then realizing her feet were still bare. At least she was dressed. Her body felt loose, as if her bones had melted, and her head was full of clouds, but the pleasure Owen had given her with his mouth and his hands was already fading. There had been no time to enjoy the afterglow, or to welcome him into her arms and her body. To complete the act. She became aware that she had abandoned him as if he had meant nothing.

But she could not think of that now.

Elijah was here. Why was he here? What had happened?

Anxiously she looked about the garden but couldn't see him. The sun had warmed the herb patch, releasing spicy scents as she brushed against them. It occurred to her that this might be a trap, and that it hadn't been Elijah who asked for her but Theo. Was he hiding somewhere, about to pounce on her?

"Elijah?" she called nervously.

The touch on her shoulder made her jump and when she swung around, wide-eyed, her loose hair flying, there he was. Elijah.

At least . . . well of course it was him, but he looked so different from the handsome, animated young man who had always been full of smiles. This Elijah was ashen faced, his fair hair standing up in spikes as if he had forgotten to comb it, and his blue eyes glassy with tears. He looked as if he hadn't smiled since Archie died.

"Ellis," he croaked, and then with a sob, wrapped his arms around her and held her tight.

She hugged him back, feeling the familiar hard warmth of his body, and the trembling of his shoulders as he wept. Suddenly, she was back in Breamore, standing at Archie's bedside where her husband lay still and cold. It was a moment before she realized how thin Elijah had become, as if he had stopped eating.

"What has happened?" she asked when he had cried himself to a standstill. She tried to see his face, but he only buried it deeper into her shoulder, and tightened his grip on her as if he did not want to let her go. "Elijah? Please. Tell me what's happened."

He finally raised his head. They were much the same height, and she saw that his face was flushed and tear-stained, and his eyes were red and swollen with weeping.

"Archie is gone. I'll never see him again. How can I bear it, Ellis? Why didn't I die, too?"

The soft lilt of his voice was so familiar, so dear. Ellis felt her tears overflow to join his. "What of Theo?" she burst out, fear clenching inside her.

His face twisted in fury. "I hate him," he hissed. "He's been looking for me. He came to the village and searched the houses, but I hid in a cellar. I knew he'd be back. Rowan found me and took me into the forest. Rowan knows places no one else does, and he said I'd be safe for a while."

Ellis's shoulders sagged with relief. "Good, that is good, Elijah. I was so worried about you." She had been right about Theo's unrelenting need for vengeance when it came to Archie and his sweetheart. "And Rowan. Where *is* Rowan?" She looked about, as if expecting to see his craggy face pop up from behind a shrub.

"He's over there." Elijah pointed toward the trees. "He's keeping watch, just in case. He said he saw you a few days ago, right here in the garden. He was so excited, Ellis," and he smiled despite his woebegone face. "That's how I knew where to come to find you."

"I'm glad."

"He told me what happened when you tried to escape in the coach. How Theo followed you and sought to take you back to Breamore. Or worse." His blue eyes had never looked more serious.

"Theo has been here," Ellis said. "He was at the door, asking if I was inside. He wanted to search the house, but Owen . . . Lord Lyndhurst, sent him away. So far, he hasn't come back. Maybe he's given up."

But Elijah shook his head, and his next words dashed her hopes. "He'll come back. He will keep looking until he finds us."

She didn't know what to say. Ellis had been pretending she was safe here at Hawthorne Lodge, and it had taken Elijah's grim prediction to puncture her bubble.

Suddenly Daffyd the peacock gave a loud shriek. They both jumped, and then laughed when they realized what it was, but the respite was brief. Elijah tipped his head to the side, and took her in, as if only just seeing her mermaid dress and her wild hair.

"You look . . ."

She felt awkward to admit in the face of Elijah's grief that she was happy here. Or at least she had been until the spectre of Theo had raised its head again. But she didn't have to say anything, because Elijah gripped her hands in his, and when he spoke again his voice was urgent.

"I am going west, to the mountains. Rowan has family there and we can hide where Theo will never find us. That's why I came here to talk to you, Ellis. Will you come with us?"

Ellis opened her mouth and closed it again. She pictured herself hiding in the bleak mountains, huddled by a fire, and sleeping in a cottage while listening, always listening, for Theo to find them. She would almost rather walk up the long driveway to Breamore than do that.

And what of Owen? If she left with Elijah and Rowan, she would never see him again. Owen, with his earnestness and his bright eyes and his quick, wicked smile, and the way he had kissed her and touched her . . . was it only moments ago? She remembered again how she had rushed out of the room and left him. What must he think of her? The look on his face when he'd heard Elijah was at the door . . .

Owen had wanted to know the truth—*I wish I knew what you were*—and she hadn't been able to bring herself to answer.

She must tell him everything. She must! Ellis no longer believed Owen would give her away to Theo. Although she *did* fear he would want nothing more to do with her. He was attracted to humble Ellis Mallory, but what would he think when he discovered she was the Dowager Duchess of Breamore? With her life in danger she might be more trouble to him than she was worth. She did not think he would betray her, never that, but he might well bundle her into a coach for London and think himself well rid of her.

Then she would never see him again, and that was too awful for her to bear.

"What is it?" Elijah asked sharply, seeing her distress. "Ellis?"

Ellis glanced over her shoulder at the house, belatedly remembering the window in Owen's study that looked out over the garden. But there was nothing to see, only the reflection of flowers and sky in the glass pane. Owen wouldn't be looking out anyway, he would be working on his drawings to prepare them for publication. Or was he sketching a depiction of what they had just done? Drawing it from memory to add to the series his publisher wanted from him.

He saw Ellis as a means to an end, but she could not bear to leave him. Not yet.

"You must go," she said to Elijah. "I want you to. I need to know you are safe."

He was still watching her doubtfully. "What about you?"

"I will go to London. To my mother. Lord Lyndhurst says he

will arrange it."

"And you trust him? Lord Lyndhurst?"

"Yes, I do."

There must have been some giveaway in her voice, because the old sparkle of humor flickered in Elijah's eyes. "I hope he is good enough for you," he said quietly. "Otherwise, I will have words with him." Then his mouth trembled. "I wish . . ." he began, but could not finish.

Ellis hugged him again, kissing his cheek and his hair as he bowed his head before her. "I *will* see you again," she said firmly. "When this is over and I have dealt with Theo, I will send for you and Rowan. We will live at Breamore again, I promise."

He took a shaky breath and managed to smile before he turned and began to walk from the garden. Ellis stood and watched, and as he reached the fields he broke into a loping run. The forest loomed before him, and a shadow stepped from the trees and moved to meet him. Rowan. The two men turned and lifted their hands in farewell. A moment later the trees seemed to swallow them up and they were gone.

Chapter Fifteen

OWEN HAD STOOD before the window, frozen to the spot, as Ellis had embraced the stranger. He had felt as if he had a fever, his blood at boiling point as he watched them hug and kiss. It was obvious there was a deep affection between them. Perhaps they were lovers, and Ellis had been separated from him by circumstance or disapproving relatives. Was that why she was fleeing by coach in the forest—if indeed there *was* a coach, he reminded himself.

And now this man, this Elijah Jones, had found her. Why had he just walked away? Had they decided their love could not survive whatever it was that had come between them? Or had Ellis promised to meet him elsewhere so that they could continue their love affair in safety?

He was speculating like a fool, but he did not think it was entirely speculation. He had borne witness to the attachment between Ellis and Elijah, and even a blind man could see that whatever game Ellis had been playing with him, her real loyalty, her real love, was for Elijah.

Too many questions without answers. Too many wild thoughts spinning in his head. Despite Ellis's secrets he had begun to feel as if he knew her, that he was falling in love with her, and now . . .

He just wished it did not hurt so much.

For all his talk of acting professionally and of gentlemanly behavior, he could admit that he had begun to crave more. A relationship, where he could freely kiss her and hold her and take her to his bed. Had he been falling in love with her? Well, now that lay in pieces. She had maneuvered him and tricked him and almost persuaded him she wanted him as much as he wanted her.

He felt lower than he had ever felt, and angrier than he could ever remember being, and oh so jealous.

He looked down and realized he had crumpled up the latest sketch in his closed fist, too upset to know what he was doing. For an instant he was tempted to tear it in two. How good that would feel! At least for a minute or two. But common sense came to his rescue, and he smoothed it out with care, and then placed it between the leaves of a large book to flatten it again. Whatever Owen's inner turmoil, he had a job to do. Hugh Madrigal was waiting for this new series of drawings and Owen refused to let him down. He refused to allow Ellis Mallory to break him.

And if the worst came to the worst and she left, there were plenty of other pretty girls who would be happy to sit for him.

The outside door closed. He waited, wondering if she would have the audacity to walk back into the room as if nothing had happened. When he heard her on the stairs and knew she wasn't coming back, he wasn't sure whether to be outraged or wretched.

After an indeterminate time staring into space, Owen sat down at his desk and began to work again, shutting away his reeling thoughts and bruised heart. He scoffed at his earlier idea that he had fallen in love with her. How could he have? He had only known her for such a short time. Love grew slowly and steadily, not like this feeling, this whirlwind of painful emotion that made his hands shake and his eyes sting.

It was lust, pure and simple, but he was certain that whatever game she was playing, Ellis had felt it, too. She had wanted him, she'd told him so, and if they hadn't been interrupted he would have taken her.

The afternoon light faded into evening, and soon Polly was at the door, informing him that their meal was ready. "Joan has cooked your favorite!"

Owen couldn't even remember what his "favorite" was but found himself rising and going to his room to wash and shave before he changed his clothes. He did it automatically, without thought. He could have stayed upstairs or locked himself in his study, but it seemed more important to show Ellis that he wasn't affected by her lies.

Before he knew it, he was seated at the table in the dining room.

Ellis arrived shortly afterward. He gave her a brief glance and thought she looked pale, her face strained, as though the skin had tightened over her bones. Her hair was neatly coiled on her crown and her clothing was modest—a blue gown with a high collar and sleeves gathered at her wrists. It was a far cry from the outfits she had worn as his model, and it felt as if she was marking a line between the two.

She gave him a nod as she sat down, and a moment later Joan came to serve them.

His housekeeper was also quiet, her suspicious gaze going from Owen to Ellis and back again. Her mouth was pinched shut, as if there was a great deal she wanted to say but was restraining herself. Owen was grateful for that—the last thing he needed was one of Joan's lectures. When she left them alone, he pretended to eat, and by the way in which Ellis was arranging and rearranging her food, he guessed she was pretending, too.

Until she set down her cutlery with a clatter and looked up at him.

"Owen," she said. "I want to talk to you."

"Talk to me," he said, purposely brusque, loading up his fork again with whatever was on his plate. "What about?"

"The man who came to see me. Elijah." She sounded frustrated and worried.

"What of him?" He lifted his gaze, making sure it was cold

and disinterested, because that was the only way he could protect himself from the emotional damage she was inflicting on him. "Is he going to interfere with you sitting for me?"

Was that hurt in her dark eyes? She must be playing with him. Owen refused to imagine she was genuinely pained by his response.

"No," she said. "But I want to explain—"

"No need," he said in that same cold voice. "I don't need to know your private affairs. We will finish the drawings and then I will put you on a coach for London. That was our deal, was it not?"

He chewed, swallowed, and loaded his fork again with precise movements.

Ellis took some time to answer, but he kept his eyes down, busily cutting up his meat into bite-sized pieces that he had no intention of eating.

"Yes." She spoke at last, her voice huskier than usual. "You're quite right. That was our deal. But Owen—"

"Then there's nothing more to be said." He took another mouthful despite the food almost choking him.

He half thought she would argue with him and wasn't sure whether to be disappointed or relieved when, after a long moment, Ellis began to eat, too.

They finished the meal in silence, the only interruptions being when Joan and Polly cleared the plates and brought in pudding. Even the two women seemed oddly reticent, as if they were affected by the uncomfortable atmosphere in the room. Normally Owen and Ellis would be chatting politely, and even if was only the weather they were discussing, it had been comfortable.

But not now.

When they were done—had a meal ever before taken so bloody long?—Ellis rose. "I am going to retire," she announced. "I am tired."

She hesitated as if waiting for him to reply, and he felt her eyes on his bent head as he played with the barely eaten apple crumble.

"Goodnight," he said as pleasantly as he could manage.

"Owen," her voice was uncertain, "I've enjoyed spending time with you. Whatever you might think of me, I have rarely enjoyed anything as much. But I think I should leave tomorrow. Unless you want me to stay?"

The hopeful note in her voice almost broke him, but he remained stoic. "You must do as you wish," he said, as if he was indifferent to her.

She nodded. Was that a tear spilling down her cheek? Manipulation, his brain said. Merrily had cried at will. Before he could move or speak again, the door closed behind her.

Owen dropped the spoon and clasped his head in his hands. He was a fool. Why had he allowed himself to fall under her spell? After Merrily he should have known better. He had thought himself to be more sensible, more pragmatic than that, and instead he had made an even worse hash of it with Ellis.

He didn't realize Joan had come in to clear the dishes until she spoke.

"You know I am your greatest devotee," she said gently.

Owen looked up warily. He had thought he had avoided the lecture, but it seemed his relief was premature. "Please, Joan, not now."

"Yes, now," she retorted. "You need to hear this, my lord."

He sighed and leaned back in his chair, pushing away the pudding. "I'm sure you will not tell me anything I don't already know. I have been a fool. You'd think I would have known better after Merrily, but instead I let myself fall for the lies of the very next woman who came to my door."

"Ellis isn't Merrily."

Surprised, Owen let himself look at her. She appeared very solemn. "No? They are both liars. You warned me."

"She *is* lying but I don't think it's to do you mischief," she said. "She's afraid. Elijah Jones, the man who came to the door, is also afraid. Although I don't know him, I know his family in the village, and they are good, honest folk. He has been a servant at Breamore for years, and there has never been a bad word spoken about him." Then, her eyes narrowing, "Did you think he and Ellis were lovers? You've got the wrong end of the stick there . . . sir. Elijah doesn't lie down with women. Just as I don't lie down with men."

Owen blinked. "He doesn't . . . oh!"

"They are friends, from what I gathered. And they are in trouble. The coach, the highwayman—I may not have found any evidence of either, but that doesn't mean it isn't true. Ellis has stayed here with us because she is frightened, but also because she feels safe at the Lodge. She feels safe with *you*, my lord."

"I should have asked her for the truth, but I could see she didn't trust me, and I didn't want to drive her away. Selfish of me, I know, but my drawings of her are the best I have ever done."

Joan smiled as if she couldn't help herself. He saw movement near the open door and realized Polly was there. For support he supposed. "You may as well come in and have your halfpenny's worth, too," he muttered.

Polly grinned and then bit her lip. "Sorry. Joan was worried you'd give her notice, and I couldn't let her leave without me. But she's right, sir. Ellis is in some sort of trouble, but she's stayed here because she can't bring herself to leave."

"Well, she seems to have won both of you over," he muttered.

The two women exchanged a glance. "She's the sort of person you can't help but like," Polly said.

"And now I've told her she's getting on the coach tomorrow." He shook his head. God he was a fool. Sulking like a child because he thought she didn't love him. Owen had believed himself better than that, but it seemed where Ellis Mallory was concerned he had reverted to childhood.

He could pretend this was all about his drawings and not being able to complete the series, but that wasn't really the problem. Owen needed her. He *wanted* her to stay. In the short time she had been at Hawthorne Lodge, she had become the reason he couldn't sleep at night. And the reason he got up in the morning.

"What should I do?" He put his head in his hands. "You are both so full of suggestions, tell me that."

He felt two hands, one on each shoulder. Joan said, "Go and tell her you didn't mean it." While at the same time Polly said, "Ask her to stay!"

Pushing up clumsily from his seat, his chair almost tipping over, Owen stumbled out of the room.

He took the stairs two at a time with a terrible urgency. He knew he should stop and think, consider his actions, but he didn't want to think. He dared not think. If he stopped and thought, he would lose her.

The door to Ellis's bedchamber was closed but he knocked hard upon it. There was movement inside, footsteps, and then she opened the door a crack and peered out. Her dark eyes grew big with surprise.

"Owen? What is it? Has something happened?"

He'd frightened her, and that was the last thing he'd wanted to do.

"I'm sorry," he said, running a hand through his unruly curls. "I don't know what came over me." Well, that wasn't exactly true. "I mean . . . seeing you with that man, I just couldn't think straight."

She searched his face before comprehension filled her own. "Oh. The window. You saw me and Elijah."

"Yes, I saw you and Elijah," he agreed. He reached out and cupped her cheek in his palm. "Can I come in? I know I said I didn't want to talk, but I do."

She hesitated and he dropped his hand. She had decided he wasn't worth bothering about. His heart sank, but then she widened the door, and gratefully Owen stepped inside. He wasn't looking at the room or anything in it, he was looking at Ellis. She was twisting her hands together as if this conversation was difficult for her.

"Elijah and I are friends," she said quietly. "We've been through a difficult time together. I was worried about him, and he was worried about me. He wanted me to leave Hawthorne Lodge and come with him."

"Leave?" This time he covered her hands with his own and looked down into her worried face. "No, please don't. I don't want you to. Stay here with me, at least for a bit longer."

"I should go. What if I put you in danger?"

Owen snorted a reckless laugh. "I can deal with any danger that comes my way." But he wondered if that was true. Certainly, he could put up a fight, but he was an artist, not a pugilist. Wryly, he remembered that it had been the mention of his uncle that had sent off the man demanding entry to the Lodge, and nothing to do with his fearsome demeanour.

But Ellis seemed to take his words at face value, and her tension eased. She gave a sad little smile. "If I left now, I would miss you. So much."

"I would miss you, too," he said, and found he could not look away from her, their eyes meeting and saying things that needed no words.

And then he, or she, or maybe both, reached for each other, and they were kissing. Her arms were twined around his neck, tangled in his hair, and he held her so close that their bodies seemed to merge.

Owen knew then he was completely lost, there was no going back, and he found that he didn't care.

Chapter Sixteen

ELLIS HAD WANTED this so much, nearly from the first moment she had seen Owen. Even before she had kissed him and the taste and smell and feel of him made her ache with longing. It was as if of all the men in the world, her heart and her mind had already known this was the one for her.

He was still kissing her, his mouth against her throat, his curls tickling her nose as he bent his head. Perhaps he liked the smell and taste and feel of her, as much as she did him. He was no longer a principled gentleman keeping his distance—he was a man who was insatiable for her.

Suddenly he swung her up into his arms and she gave a squeak. He was carrying her, his intent gaze on hers as if all he could see was her, and then he lay her carefully down on the bed. She thought that might be it, that he would pull back and wish her goodnight, but instead he stretched out beside her, and nuzzled against her, breathing on her skin, and pushing aside her gown and letting his teeth graze her collarbone.

"I want to learn everything about you," he whispered. "I want to kiss every inch of you."

"Every inch?" she gasped. "I want to do the same." Then, hurriedly, "I'm sorry I left you before. To go to Elijah. I wouldn't have if it weren't—"

He stopped her with a kiss, his lips firm against hers, and then the tip of his tongue tracing their shape. As she responded, he deepened the kiss until she couldn't remember what she was going to say.

He stripped the gown from her body and his lips were on her breasts, his hands caressing the rounded flesh, and they both groaned. His mouth sucking on her nipple was so exquisite she could hardly breathe. The pleasure produced a desperate ache that was linked to the flesh between her thighs, a memory of the pleasure he had brought her earlier.

Had she ever wondered if reality would be a pale imitation of her imagination and the romances she read? Well she knew now. Reality was so much better, or perhaps it was just that Owen made it so.

"Let me look at you, too," she gasped, her hands beneath his shirt, exploring his warm skin. In response he shrugged the garment off over his head and tossed it aside. She clung to the firm muscles of his upper arms, before sliding her hands over his shoulders, and leaning in to press her lips to the hollow of his throat. Owen was lean and hard-bodied—she could see his bones beneath the muscle and skin—but he was made that way. A healthy male animal whose long body seemed so perfect to her. He used that word often when it came to Ellis, but right now he was the one who deserved it.

He was struggling to unfasten his breeches, and she reached to help, making it worse. Their fingers getting in each other's way. They laughed, and he kissed her again, seeming to lose himself for a time. Eventually, he tugged the garment down and threw it after his shirt. That made her laugh, too. She was giddy with joy.

And then she stopped, and her eyes widened. She had seen him half naked on the chaise longue today, but she had been at such a fever pitch she had barely been able to think straight. This was different, and she looked her fill.

Her gaze fixed on his shaft, rising out of the dark curls at his groin, and angling upward against his belly. She reached out to stroke her finger down its length, and then up again. There was a milky drop leaking from the tip, and she circled it around the head of his cock.

That made him groan, and once again he leaned in to capture her mouth with his, pressing her back into the soft bed.

She wanted him, all of him. His body on hers, his mouth on hers. He reached for her hips, and his hands slid around to clasp the globes of her bottom. His body felt heavy and unfamiliar on hers, as he settled between her thighs. She was aware of his cock seeking entry, and suddenly this was all very real.

Ellis didn't mean to tense, but she was a virgin. An eager one, it was true, but still inexperienced apart from the basic mechanics of what was about to happen. Owen must have felt her sudden rigidity because he stopped moving.

"Ellis?" His voice was deep and very close to her ear. "Is this too fast for you, *cariad*? I can go slower. I can wait. We have all the time in the world."

But did they? For all she knew Theo might be approaching the door now, to demand to be allowed inside, and Ellis could not risk that. She wanted Owen, all of him, so why did she suddenly have these foolish doubts?

"Ellis?" he murmured. "Tell me what's wrong."

There had been enough deceit on her part. She took a shaky breath.

"I've never done this before. But I want to. So much, Owen."

Now *he* tensed, and she could sense his indecision in the hitching of his breath. He lifted his weight off her. Was this it? Was he going to stop now? Warily, she opened her eyes and looked up at where he was hovering above her. He seemed to be considering having a chivalrous discussion with her, and she really couldn't let him talk them both out of this moment.

"I want this," she said, stretching up to kiss his jaw, the corner of his mouth. She tried to tug him back down. "I want you."

Briefly, he resisted. "Are you sure?"

"Yes, yes, I'm sure!"

Now he was smiling, and she felt the curve of his lips with hers. "I won't hurt you," he promised earnestly.

"You would never hurt me," she whispered.

Carefully, he lowered himself back between her thighs, and she felt his cockhead against her soft flesh. He was kissing her again, deep, passionate kisses that distracted her from the pressure of his entry. His hand cupped her breast, tweaking the hard nipple, and pleasure soared through her.

He was deeper inside her now, but when he moved his length rubbed against her lower lips, parting them and finding that aching pearl. She arched into him with a soft cry. What had been a tingle of pleasure turned into a raging torrent.

This felt right, it felt perfect.

His was licking her throat, tasting and nuzzling, and she stretched so that he had better access. She could feel him fully inside her now, stretching her, and then he reached down to circle his thumb against her swollen flesh, and the pleasure seemed to build and build.

"Want you so much," he mumbled against her, his free arm caging her, his hips rocking, until she felt surrounded by him.

"Yes, yes . . ." She kept speaking but it was just nonsense. Her entire being was focused on that point of contact, his body sliding into hers, his thumb lifting her higher and then . . . she cried out as everything shattered.

Ellis wasn't sure how long she lay there before he cried out as he reached his own peak. He was talking nonsense, too, and kissing her wildly. It felt as if she was being buffeted by a storm, and pleasure speared through her for a second time. She had not expected that. Although not as tumultuous as the first climax, it was long and slow and rather wonderful. Eventually, she reached the eye of the storm, and everything stilled. Her heartbeat slowed and her breaths returned to normal.

Owen lifted his head, his face flushed, his hair damp from exertion and his bright hazel eyes delving into hers. "Are you—"

"I feel wonderful."

He grinned. "So do I. That was . . . I've never felt like this," he admitted, and she could hear the wonder in his voice.

Ellis stroked his cheek, learning the shape of his face, feeling the smooth-shaven skin of his jaw. "I've been so alone all my life," she said. "There have been friends, and I have my family, but inside I always felt a loneliness. Now you are there."

He kissed her tenderly and when he moved to lie on his side, their faces barely inches apart, he smiled.

Ellis's eyelids felt heavy, but she reminded herself she needed to speak to him. It was past time she told him the whole truth.

"I want to explain to you—" she began.

Gently he pressed his fingertips to her lips. "In the morning," he said. "You can tell me everything then."

Ellis was too grateful to protest, though it came with a measure of guilt. She could put it off for a little longer. Surely the morning would be soon enough to confess all she had been keeping from him. She hoped it would make no difference, and right now she felt as if they could overcome any hurdle. That together they were invincible.

Her eyes closed and she fell asleep to Owen's gentle smile and his hand tenderly stroking her face.

Chapter Seventeen

O WEN SAT UP and yawned. He had been awoken by a noise outside. It sounded like a coach arriving, followed by voices. Naked, he rose from the bed, and padded over to the window to peer out. But he had forgotten Ellis's bedchamber overlooked the back of the Lodge, and although he could still hear the commotion, he could not see anything.

He sighed. He would have much preferred to stay right where he was for the rest of the day, instead of bothering with unwelcome guests. His sketchbook was on the bedside table, and he glanced back at it with a smile. Ellis had been asleep when he had drawn her, lovingly reproducing her long lashes and her closed eyes, her lips parted slightly as she dreamed. She'd thrown off the covers, her body laid out like a banquet on the bed, and he had taken full advantage as his drawing took shape.

Owen would never use this in the book, in any book. It was private, for him alone, the memory of a memorable night.

As he had finished the drawing she had stirred and smiled up at him. Before he knew it he had found himself fully erect, and urgently in need of her again. He could have restrained himself—he was prepared to wait if she didn't want them to join together so soon after her first time—but she had reached out to take his hand in hers.

"Are you sure?" he had asked, ready to list all the reasons she should refuse him.

"Owen, I have never been more certain," she had responded, teasingly.

So he had climbed onto the bed and kissed her soft breasts, lathing the flushed tips with his tongue until she was clinging to him. Then he had moved down to the soft, delicious flesh between her thighs. She had moaned and arched against him, as he had sucked and kissed her, bringing her to another powerful climax.

Afterward, she had welcomed him into her body, wrapping her legs around his hips, meeting his every thrust. He had felt as if he were flying, up over the Lodge and the fields and the forest, up toward the stars. Even when his climax began to fade and they had both fallen back to sleep, he had felt as light as a feather, and full of a marvellous sense of joy.

The noise outside wasn't going away—if anything it was getting louder—and Owen realized he knew one of the voices. Downstairs he heard the rattle of the bolt on the front door, and Joan's cry of pleasure.

Uncle Steven, Viscount Hawthorne, had come for a visit.

He moved to the bed to wake Ellis again and found her already sitting up. Her dark hair cascaded around her nakedness, and she pushed it back over her shoulders and blinked at him sleepily.

If I could wake up to her every morning for the rest of my life, I would be a very happy man.

The thought popped into his head, but when the questions and then the doubts tried to follow, he refused to let them in. He and Ellis needed to talk, just the two of them, but that could come later. After he had greeted his uncle.

"Who is that?" Her dark eyes had widened, and he saw her muscles strain, as if at any moment she would leap up and run.

"Only my uncle." Owen sat down at her side and reached for her hand, kissing her fingers. "Nothing to be worried about." He added with a wry smile, "I should go down and greet him."

"Your uncle? The viscount?" She was properly awake now, gripping his hand tightly as she came up to kneel beside him.

He was too distracted by her slender body to answer. He wanted to climb back into bed with her and lock the door, and bedamned to his uncle. Although the viscount was known for his impromptu visits to his nephew, why had he chosen *now* to call?

She wrapped her arms about his neck, and pressed her lips to his cheek, before claiming his mouth again.

Owen groaned. "Mm, wish I could stay."

She laughed softly and clung a moment more, her curves soft on his body, before letting him go with obvious reluctance.

With a last, lingering kiss, Owen began to dress. "I'll send Polly to you," he said. "When you're ready, come down and I'll introduce you."

As Owen closed the door, he was feverishly reminding himself that his uncle never stayed long when he visited. Then he felt ashamed. He and his uncle were close, and while he was here he deserved Owen's full attention. If it weren't for this new turn in his relationship with Ellis, he would have been glad to see the elderly gentleman.

He *was* glad to see him.

He met Polly bustling up the stairs as he was going down. She gave him a sly smile as he informed her that Ellis was awake, but he didn't stop to hear her thoughts on this new, happy state of affairs. As he approached the breakfast room, he could hear his uncle and Joan sharing pleasantries.

The viscount started toward Owen as soon as he saw him with a cry of, "My dear boy!"

Viscount Hawthorne was a short, rotund gentleman with a bald pate and tufts of grey hair above his ears. He was as physically different from Owen as it was possible to be, apart from his eyes, which were the same hazel color as Owen's.

Now he reached to take Owen's hands, holding them in a firm grip as he smiled warmly up into his taller nephew's face.

"My dear boy!" he exclaimed again. "I feel like I haven't seen you for ages. Why don't you come to London more often?"

Owen grinned back at him. His uncle's enthusiasm never failed to move him. They were the only two of their family surviving and sometimes his uncle became quite sentimental about it.

"I don't come to London because I am perfectly happy here," Owen replied, just as he always did.

"Lord Lyndhurst is well looked after," Joan interrupted, busily setting out the chafing dishes on the sideboard. The smell of sausages, bacon, eggs, and toast filled the air.

Viscount Hawthorne joined her, rubbing his hands together with glee.

"Is Miss Mallory joining us this morning?" Joan asked blithely, but her glance to Owen was curious.

"Yes, she will be down shortly," he said, then wondered if he should have pretended not to know. His answer had been a bit of a giveaway.

His uncle had turned to look at him with interest. "And *who* is Miss Mallory?"

"My new model," he said quickly.

Joan opened her mouth to add to that but closed it again when Owen shot her a warning look.

"I thought your model was called Merrily," the viscount responded, beginning to fill his plate.

"Merrily left for greener pastures," Owen said, also reaching for a plate. He was hungry, which was not surprising when he remembered last night.

Did he need to tell his uncle that Ellis was more than just sitting for him? Was it too soon to disclose that he thought he was in love? He wasn't sure how the viscount would take the surprising news. Although Owen knew he would be supportive, would he be pleased? Uncle Steven had hinted at various times that he hoped Owen would marry a titled lady, if he was inclined to marry at all.

And why was he suddenly thinking about marriage when all he wanted to do was enjoy the moment?

There was a step in the doorway, the rustle of skirts, and there she was. Ellis was wearing the respectable gown with the white skirt and green bodice, the matching ribbon tied precisely under her breasts. She caught his glance, her cheeks faintly flushed, and then her dark eyes darted to the viscount. And grew bigger.

Remembering his manners, Owen made the introductions. "Uncle Steven, this is Miss Ellis Mallory, my . . ." He paused on her description, but he could hardly say "the love of my life," could he? At least, not without discussing it with Ellis first. He settled on, "She has kindly agreed to sit for me. Ellis this is my uncle, Viscount Hawthorne."

The two of them were still looking at each other, and as the silence lingered, so Owen's misgivings grew. His uncle's open, friendly face was creased in a frown, and Ellis's smile had disappeared. In fact, she looked . . . afraid.

Owen moved closer to her, feeling the need to protect her. "What is it?" he asked sharply, looking from one to the other. "Uncle? Ellis?"

"Miss Mallory?" the viscount repeated slowly. He gave Owen a bewildered look. "My dear boy, either my eyesight is failing me spectacularly or this is the Duchess of Breamore."

Ellis's body felt rigid beside Owen. Her eyes flicked to him and then back to the viscount as if she didn't want to read what was in Owen's face. He was still expecting her to refute the claim when she sighed.

"You are correct, Viscount Hawthorne. At least . . . I am now the *Dowager* Duchess of Breamore."

Dowager Duchess? Owen opened his mouth but wasn't sure what to say. He certainly didn't know what to think. Ellis Mallory was a duchess, a married woman? A widow? He suddenly remembered the torn black dress she had worn when she had arrived at his door. He had thought she was in mourning for her father, not her husband. And then, a clearer memory, last night when they had made love and she had said it was her first time. There was no mistaking that. She was a virgin. Then how could she be a widow?

Uncle Steven was nodding sombrely. "My condolences on the death of your husband, Your Grace," he said gently. "He seemed a jolly fellow on the few occasions I met him."

She nodded graciously. Regally. Just like a duchess. "Thank you."

Owen gaped. He *knew* he shouldn't feel as if he'd been lied to. It was his own fault, wasn't it, that he didn't know the full story? He hadn't wanted to listen. Although she could have given him a hint, and then he would not feel so . . . *deceived*. This wasn't a small thing, a little white fib about her past. All this time he had thought she was simple Miss Mallory and treated her as such, and she was a duchess.

Last night he had lain with Ellis, a woman he thought himself in love with, and this morning he was presented with the Dowager Duchess of Breamore.

Reluctantly his gaze met hers, and he saw the pleading in her dark eyes. She wanted him to understand, to forgive, and right now Owen wasn't sure he could.

"There was a whisper making the rounds when I left London." His uncle was still talking, and if he was aware of the tension in the room, he was choosing to ignore it. "There was speculation that because no one had seen you for several days now that you had disappeared. I am very glad to see the talk has no basis in fact, and that you are safe and well here at Hawthorne Lodge. With my nephew." His eyebrows rose questioningly.

Ellis seemed to be struggling to find an answer. "I did disappear," she said at last. "But there is a very good reason for me doing so. I was in danger and Owen . . . Lord Lyndhurst took me in and kept me safe."

"Safe?" The viscount frowned. "Safe from what? Or should I say from whom? The whispers I mentioned spoke of the duke's cousin, Sir Theo Abergele."

Owen couldn't keep silent any longer. "Is that the man who came to the door?" he demanded. "The one who caused your coach accident when he was pursuing you?"

The idea of Ellis being in such a precarious position made him angry, and his anger overcame his hurt about her hiding so many truths from him.

"Yes," she said, once again meeting his eyes with her own, a myriad of emotions in their dark depths. "Theo has many friends, and I wasn't sure who I could trust."

"You can trust my uncle, and you can trust *me*."

He had hardly finished speaking when she blurted out, "Theo wanted me to marry him. It was a simple way of ensuring he would inherit everything. I refused. I couldn't marry him. He's vile. But once I had refused, there was only one way he could claim Breamore under the terms of my husband's will, and that was if I was dead."

"The devil!" Uncle Steven exclaimed.

"My groom and I decided on a plan. I would pretend to pay a call on a neighbor, but once away from Breamore we would make our way with haste to London. But Theo knew what we were up to, and he followed us. That is why I was in the forest, and why I came to Lord Lyndhurst's door. If it weren't for him keeping me safe Theo would have me now."

Owen was speechless. His head felt as if it was full of stampeding horses, and he could hear his heart pounding in his ears. "We should confront this man!" he said furiously.

The other two stared at him, and it was only then he realized his teeth were gritted and his hands clenched into fists, and he must have seemed far from his usual mild self.

His uncle frowned. "Not sure that would be such a good idea, nephew. It would only give Sir Theo warning that we know what he is up to and therefore put the duchess in greater danger."

"And it would put Owen in danger, too," Ellis said.

Before Owen could inform them that he didn't give a jot

about that, his uncle took the floor once again.

"However, I *do* have an idea. I am acquainted with a man in London who may be able to help Your Grace. His name is Nicholas Blake, and he specialises in tricky situations like this."

"Please, call me Ellis. And I am very grateful for any help you can give. I realize now how selfish I have been staying here at Hawthorne Lodge. It was just . . ." She chewed on her lip. "It was so lovely not to have to worry about things for a little while."

The viscount smiled, and Owen could see his uncle was already won over.

"Where can I find this Nicholas Blake?" Ellis said.

"Never you mind about that. I will take you to him. Pack what you need, and we will set off today. But first," he said with a grin, "I desire to sit down to Joan's exceptional breakfast."

Ellis didn't seem to know what to say. She looked down and then up again, her gaze going from one to the other. "Thank you. You are very kind. You are *both* very kind."

Was Owen kind? He wasn't sure. His head was a confused mess of thoughts and his heart a jumble of feelings. "Uncle, are you sure it wouldn't be better to stay here? Ellis is safe here, and we can protect her. I refuse to believe there is any danger we cannot deal with."

The viscount gave him another hearty slap on the back. "That is all very well, my boy, but this villain has tentacles all over the country. I know him well enough to fear he will find some way to spirit the duchess away and we won't be able to stop him. London and Nicholas Blake are our best option."

Joan interrupted them then with yet more food, and the viscount made haste to sit down at the table with his loaded plate.

"Remind me why I ever let you leave my house in London," he said to the housekeeper, spearing a sausage with his fork.

Joan smiled. "I'm sure you do very well in London, sir. And if you miss my cooking then you should visit us more often."

The viscount didn't reply. He was already tucking in.

Before Ellis could sit down, Owen took hold of her hand.

"Can we talk for a moment?" he asked quietly. He hadn't thought his uncle heard, but of course he did.

"You talk all you want, my boy, but be quick if you want to partake of this magnificent repast. I have a hearty appetite this morning!"

Ellis smiled. She obviously found the viscount delightful, and in other circumstances Owen would have been pleased they were getting on with each other. But right now he needed to speak with her alone.

He led her into his study and closed the door. Light was beaming through the window, turning everything to gold, and as she stood in the glow, Owen could not help but be struck once more by her beauty. He also could not help but wonder what would happen when they reached London, because there was no way on earth he was staying behind. But how could he remain at her side and keep her safe? She would no longer be Ellis Mallory, but the Dowager Duchess of Breamore, one of the highest peeresses in the land, and well beyond his reach. He may be a lord, but he could not even expect to sit at the same table as her.

"Owen?" She was watching him apprehensively, as if she thought he might be glad to see the back of her. "What is it you want to say?"

"Did you really think you were selfish to stay here?" he asked. "I rather think *I* was being selfish wanting you to stay just so I could use you for my drawings."

"I *loved* you drawing me," she said gravely. "The reason I wanted to stay here with you wasn't just because I felt safe. It was because I enjoyed your company. All the same it was wrong. I should have been open and honest with you, but I was afraid. Dealing with Theo made me suspicious of everybody."

"I understand," he said, although he wasn't entirely sure he did. He considered his next words, but there was no polite way to say them. "Last night when we lay together . . . it was your first time, Ellis, and yet you were a married woman! I don't understand. I can't believe your husband was unable. I did not know the Duke of Breamore personally, but I have seen him ride through the village, and he looked young and not unattractive."

He could tell she had been expecting this question. "I wanted to tell you this too, but it is complicated and there was Elijah to consider. I didn't want to put him in any more danger, even inadvertently."

"What has it to do with Elijah?"

"He and Archie were lovers. It was Elijah he would have married if he could. It was Elijah who was his true love." She hurried on as he stood in startled silence. "My marriage to Archie wasn't a real marriage, it was a sham, but I loved him all the same. Both he and Elijah were like brothers to me. For five years we were happy, until Archie died, and Theo decided he wanted it all for himself."

Her eyes filled with tears.

"I know during the sittings you didn't want to kiss me or—or touch me, but I wanted you to. I've been alone for five years and although Archie said when we married that I could take a lover, there was never anyone I wanted in that way. And then I met you. I'm sorry if you think I've been dishonest."

"You didn't exactly have to twist my arm," he retorted. She had been lonely, and Owen asking her to sit for him had opened a doorway for her to finally discover the pleasures she had been missing. That made a terrible sort of sense to him. He had been used.

"Will you—will you hold me?" A tear ran down her cheek, and she was trembling.

Owen was helpless to do other than obey. He wrapped his arms around her and held her tight against him until the trembling gradually eased.

"Will you come with me? To London?" Her breath was warm against his throat, and when he lifted his head and looked down, her lips were tantalizingly close.

"Yes," he said, powerless to refuse.

"Do you forgive me?" she asked quietly. "For keeping so

much from you?"

"Ellis, it was my fault, too, but yes, I forgive you. Do you forgive me?"

She smiled, still not moving away from him. Her long lashes lifted as she met his gaze, and she swallowed anxiously. "Perhaps, when we reach London, we could—"

But whatever it was she was about to ask was lost in his uncle's shout from the breakfast room.

"Owen! Ellis! We need to get to London. Come and eat before I polish off the entire meal."

Their laughter was rather strained, but Owen held her hand, only letting go when they entered the room. Uncle Steven looked up, a twinkle in his eye, which seemed to suggest he was well aware of the undercurrents. "There you are," he said mildly. "No dilly-dallying now."

"I think we should bring some of my servants with us, as outriders," Owen said. "Just in case we strike trouble on the journey."

His uncle nodded. "Good thinking, boy. I don't expect us to be held up—I am an important man, and even a blackguard like Sir Theo would not want to risk crossing me and upsetting my friends in the government. But we can't be certain what he might do if he is desperate enough. Best to take every precaution."

Ellis looked from one to the other of them, and Owen could already see she was more relaxed. She had shared her secrets and now it wasn't just her alone when it came to her enemy. The thought of Theo following her coach, firing at her, chasing her through the forest . . . it made him feel hot with rage and cold with fear.

He knew then he would do anything in his power to keep her safe. And although he felt fairly certain that she had taken advantage of their time together to satisfy her curiosity when it came to physical pleasures, he couldn't blame her. Her life at Breamore sounded quite lonely. However much he wished there was more to their moments of passion, he could hardly complain.

He might be disappointed and yes, hurt, but it would not stop him from doing the same thing again.

Miss Mallory he could have loved, and maybe she could have loved him, but the Dowager Duchess of Breamore was far beyond his reach. All the same, Owen knew he would be willing to give his life if it meant saving hers.

Chapter Eighteen

Ellis had not been to London for years. Not since she'd married Archie and removed to Breamore. She had never liked the society events she had been forced to attend, thrust into the midst of the *ton* like a tasty morsel for hungry mouths. Now, things were different. She was here for a reason, and she had two gentlemen who were determined to remove the threat of Theo from her life.

And one of those gentlemen she was in love with. Owen, Lord Lyndhurst, a man Theo would destroy in an instant if he learned about him. Theo wouldn't want her to find a protector, he wanted her alone and friendless. It made her determined to hide her feelings for Owen, in order to prevent anything happening to him. She would rather sacrifice herself than let Theo harm him.

Ellis had nowhere to stay in London. Archie hadn't a residence there and had been content to lease a place if he needed to spend time in the city. After his marriage he had preferred his country estate and that was where he had remained. Him and Elijah and Ellis.

Her sister Sophia's husband, the Duke of Oldney was an unpleasant fellow and Ellis had never felt welcomed by him. Nor by her sister, whose hectic social life was just the sort of existence

Ellis had always loathed. She had no wish to descend on her sister uninvited.

At first she thought that perhaps her mother might take her in, but through enquiries made by the viscount en route, they had discovered that Ellis's mother, Mrs. Mallory, was away in the north of the country with her eldest daughter Catherine. Her house was closed for the time being.

"It may not be safe for you if Sir Theo discovers you are there, alone," the viscount said. "I think the best thing is for you to come to my house and remain incognito. At least until we know what Blake has discovered. I've already sent a message ahead, and knowing him as I do, he will be busy unearthing anything that may be of use to us."

"You are putting a lot of faith in this man," Owen said, sounding unusually grumpy.

"I am, and it is justified." His uncle gave him a look of admonishment. "If I wanted to know how the government was faring, I would ask myself. If I wanted to know about the art world, or scantily clad ladies, I would ask you, my boy. If I wanted to find out what a man like Sir Theo Abergele was up to, I'd ask Blake. He is very good at his job, as you will see."

The viscount leaned closer, but his voice was just as loud. "I know you're keen to play the hero, my boy, but in such circumstances we must be clever rather than heroic."

Owen's cheeks flushed and he shot Ellis a self-conscious glance, which made her smile. Owen was such a gentleman, she understood he would want to rush to her rescue. He would do the same for any woman. She must not fool herself into thinking he had a particular partiality for her.

During the five-day journey, she had explained to Owen about her mother and sisters, and the scandal that had beset them all those years ago. Viscount Hawthorne had already heard about it, and remembered it quite well, but Owen had either forgotten or had never been interested enough to pay attention.

"When my father died and we moved to our cousin's in London, my mother was determined to see her three daughters marry well. My elder sister became engaged to a duke old enough to be her grandfather, and after that we all had to marry dukes. I was fortunate with Archie but Sophia, my next eldest sister, is married to Oldney, a man I have never liked and never trusted."

"Good God," Owen said, while his uncle snored in the corner of the coach. "That is appalling, Ellis."

"You are lucky," she told him quietly. "Your uncle was willing to let you follow your own heart when it came to your future."

He looked almost embarrassed, but she leaned across and took his hand in hers. Polly, who had accompanied them as Ellis's maid and chaperone, watched avidly. "I don't begrudge you your good fortune, Owen. Far from it. And I was hardly starving and wearing rags at Breamore. I was happy there. It just wasn't the sort of happiness I'd always dreamt of."

"If I'd known I could have visited you," Owen said.

"Archie was not on visiting terms with most of our neighbors. It was better that way. He had too much to lose."

"Of course." He looked away, and she realized he probably thought *she* would not have made him welcome. Before she could correct herself, Polly interrupted.

"I am so looking forward to seeing London. Joan says I won't like it, but I don't believe her. I want to make up my own mind."

Ellis suspected Joan might have been trying to dissuade Polly from her adventure. She was sure that the housekeeper must be missing her sweetheart, if the way in which she called out her goodbyes and waved desperately at the departing coach was any indication.

She glanced again at Owen but now he was frowning out the window.

There wasn't much private time on their journey from Wales. Polly slept in Ellis's room at the inns where they stopped, and the viscount was always present at meals or during any halts to stretch their legs. Now the doubts she had kept at bay so far rose up again as the coach wheels rumbled on. She knew Owen admired her. The night they had spent together, when he had thought her sleeping, she had heard the scratch of his pencil on paper and known he was drawing her. Was that because he had wanted to record their special moment? Or had he simply wanted another image for his book? It was a lowering thought, but did she mean nothing more to him than a pretty face?

Could he ever love her? A true love, deep love, the sort of love she had always dreamed of?

All her life Ellis had been the one to run after the others, the one left alone while her sisters voyaged off into their lives. The one no one valued quite as much. Those memories had left their mark when it came to her self-confidence.

⊰⊱⊰⊱⊰⊱

VISCOUNT HAWTHORNE'S TOWNHOUSE was not the grandest Ellis had ever seen, but grand enough for all that. As if he instinctively knew he was home, Steven woke up. He looked to his two companions and stretched and yawned, his mind already alert.

"I have been thinking," he said. "We will call you Miss Mallory for now. It is safer than declaring your true identity. You are a distant cousin. Are we agreed?"

"Agreed," Ellis said.

Next thing the door to the coach was opened and a grave gentleman in a white wig peered in at them. "My lord," he said, slight surprise in his voice. "You are back already. Was there some concern at Hawthorne Lodge?"

The viscount waved him away. "Not at all, Greenwood. My nephew decided he wanted to visit me instead, so here we are. See that his usual room is prepared for him, and another one for our guest. This is Miss Mallory, a distant cousin of my mother. We are fortunate to have her with us."

Greenwood stared without blinking. If he had any reservations about Ellis, he kept them to himself. "Very good, my lord. Does Miss Mallory know how long she will be staying with us?"

"As long as she likes," the viscount replied blithely.

Ellis could see that Viscount Hawthorne's household was run like clockwork. In no time the luggage was brought inside and carried up to their allotted rooms. When Ellis had changed with Polly's help and come downstairs again, she inquired of a servant where everyone was. She was told that the viscount had repaired to the library to write a letter, and that Owen was in the drawing room.

She went to the drawing room and found Owen standing at the window, peering out at the London scene as though he was a stranger in a strange land and was wishing himself home again. There had been little chance of a proper tête-à-tête during their journey. No chance to do any of the other wonderful things she had been longing to do with him.

This felt like the first time Ellis could say what she wanted to without being overheard by the viscount or Polly.

"Are you sorry you came?" she asked.

He spun around, his face breaking into a smile as he came to take her hands in his. "Not at all. I wanted to come. I *needed* to come."

"I hope Nicholas Blake can help me. Your uncle thinks he can."

"Uncle Steven knows a great many useful people," Owen said, watching her intently. "Do you mind staying here with us?"

"I feel safer with you and the viscount than I would if I were alone in my mother's house." She hesitated and then leaned in to kiss him.

Owen seemed surprised, but then he returned the kiss, his lips lingering. She felt a surge of desire at his touch.

"I wish we were alone," she said.

"I did think about waylaying you in one of the inns," he admitted, his voice dropping an octave, "but it was too risky. And hardly gentlemanly."

"I wish we were back at Hawthorne Lodge," she said wistfully.

"Do you?" He seemed surprised. His gaze slid over her face, as if he was trying to read the truth behind her words. As if he didn't believe her. "Breamore is a large estate . . . or so I have heard. I imagine my home seems quite small and cramped in comparison."

Did he really think that? She had worried that when he found out she was a duchess he might feel differently about her. She tried to reassure him.

"Owen, I was born a curate's daughter. We were as poor as church mice when my father died. Just because I was lucky enough to marry Archie does not mean I now desire a grand house and hundreds of sycophantic servants. I am still the same woman."

His smile was polite. Where was that wicked grin she loved so much? "I am glad to hear it. I don't have hundreds of servants, and the only sycophantic ones I employ are Joan and Polly, and they are quite enough, thank you." He hesitated, and his face grew serious. "But you are a duchess. You cannot escape that fact, no matter how poor you were as a child. Breamore belongs to you."

"I wish I *could* escape it," she said, feeling downcast. He seemed to think she was too grand for him, and she hated it. "Owen, believe me when I tell you that I have been the happiest I can ever remember being at Hawthorne Lodge. Do you think I can give up being a duchess and become Miss Mallory again?"

"Like Marie Antoinette when she played at being a milk maid?" he teased, but she could tell he did not believe such a thing was possible.

Was it worth overcoming Theo's evil designs, restoring herself to her rightful place at Breamore, only to lose the man she loved?

She rested her cheek against his shoulder, breathing in his woollen jacket and spicy soap, and after a moment his arms closed around her. Reluctantly, it seemed.

"Perhaps you can come to my room tonight?" she said boldly and held her breath for his answer.

He pressed his lips to her hair. "Your sensual adventures were cut short, weren't they? You must be disappointed. But I am not sure I should visit your room when you are a guest under my uncle's roof."

"Even if I invite you?" She added a little desperately, "Won't you need some more sketches for the rest of your series?"

She felt him go still, and when he spoke again, he sounded very formal. "You do realize I can differentiate between the fictional woman in my drawings and the real woman in my arms?"

What on earth was the matter with him? Ellis wanted to shake him. What else could she say or do to persuade him it was him she wanted? But then she wondered if he even cared. Perhaps his infatuation had run its course. She had been part of the fantasy he was creating for his publisher, and now she was a duchess in danger, and although he was tender, and willing to see she was kept safe, he did not want her in the same way he had before.

Was it over? Ellis ached at the thought. She remembered what Joan had said.

That's not to say you can't persuade him to go against his principles if you try hard enough. Although I'm not sure he will thank you for it afterward. Especially if you have some secret you haven't told him and which he will not like.

Was Joan right? She wanted to ask him but knew it was no use. Whatever had been between them had cooled, and she didn't know how to get it back. The dinner gong sounded, and Ellis smiled and moved away toward the door. "Shall we go in to dinner?"

After a moment Owen followed.

Chapter Nineteen

DINNER WAS QUIET. Even the viscount's conversation was muted, and Owen had little to say other than that he was planning to visit his publisher the next day. Ellis was about to ask him if he had brought his latest sketches with him when Greenwood interrupted them. With his white pantaloons and black tailcoat, the butler could have passed muster at a palace ball.

"There is a Mr. Blake to see you, my lord," he announced.

"Thank you, Greenwood." The viscount tossed down his napkin. "Show him into the drawing room. We will be with him shortly."

Once the door had closed again, he said, "I didn't expect him until tomorrow." He turned to Ellis. "Are you all right to speak with him, my dear? The sooner we deal with the matter of Sir Theo Abergele, the sooner you can safely return home to Breamore."

Ellis couldn't help but glance at Owen, but he was staring down at his plate. "I am very much looking forward to speaking to Mr. Blake," she replied. "All I want is for everything to go back to the way it was before."

She meant Hawthorne Lodge, but she realized too late it sounded as if she was longing to be back at Breamore with her many sycophantic servants. It was too late to correct herself, and why bother when Owen still refused to look at her?

Nicolas Blake was standing when they entered the drawing room, and Viscount Hawthorne greeted him like an old friend. He was younger than Ellis had expected, in his mid-thirties, with cropped dark hair and clever dark eyes and a dazzling smile. He was certainly a handsome specimen.

"Blake! I appreciate you responding so promptly to my request! This is my nephew, Lord Lyndhurst, and *this* is the Dowager Duchess of Breamore."

Blake greeted Ellis with a bow, those intelligent eyes running over her, while for Owen he had a slightly mocking smile. "Ah, the artist. I have heard a great deal about you from your uncle, my lord."

"And yet I have heard nothing about you," Owen said rudely.

The other man huffed a startled laugh, but the viscount clapped Owen on the back in his usual hearty manner, making Ellis wince. "Well then, you should get up to London more often, dear boy!"

"I prefer to be a country bumpkin," Owen said stubbornly.

"I have heard that, too," Blake answered dryly, before turning his attention to Ellis. "I am sorry to hear of your difficulties, Your Grace."

"Thank you. Viscount Hawthorne says you can help?"

"Yes. We will soon set matters to rights, and then you can enjoy the rest of the Season. I imagine rusticating in the country is very boring when London has so much to offer."

He shot a sideways glance at Owen, who glared back at him. The viscount appeared bemused by the antagonism between the two men, and Ellis was beginning to wonder if she would have been better off hiding in the mountains with Elijah and Rowan.

Suddenly the viscount clapped his hands loudly, making them all jump. "Enough of the pleasantries. Blake, what have you got to tell us?"

Ellis listened as Mr. Blake began to speak. "I have ascertained the contents of the duke's will. I thought it would save time. The estate was not entailed and, although the title will go to Sir Theo, everything of material value was left to you, Your Grace. If you remarry it will make no difference, except that if you die you can leave your fortune to your husband. The only other stipulations concern an Elijah Jones." He lifted his eyebrow at her in query.

"I know of them. Archie told me."

Blake nodded again but didn't ask why Elijah had been favored. Ellis decided that if Blake was as good at wheedling out information as the viscount said he was, then he probably already knew a great deal about Archie.

"There is also an addition to the will. A last-minute addendum which states that if you die a widow, then the duke's cousin, Sir Theo Abergele, gets everything."

"Archie's man of business made that change," Ellis said bitterly. "Archie trusted him, but it turned out he was more interested in what Theo could offer him."

Blake made a noncommittal noise just as Greenwood arrived with coffee.

When the cups were handed out, and they were once more alone, Ellis explained further. "Theo asked me to marry him, although he could see I was never going to accept his proposal. I think he planned to keep me a prisoner at Breamore until I agreed, but I escaped. He must have known I would try to get away from him and decided to use the situation to his own advantage by waylaying my coach. Then if I was killed, he could blame it on highwaymen and inherit Archie's title and estate without being made to look guilty of any wrongdoing."

"You did not want to marry him? Some would. It is the easier option, and after the ceremony you would not need to stay with him. You could bargain with him for a reasonable allowance and then live any life you chose and never see him again."

It sounded cold and practical, but Ellis had already spent five years of her life in a marriage that was more friendship than anything else. At least Archie and Elijah had meant her no harm.

Being married to Theo would be unbearable, and as for even the possibility of sleeping in the same bed as him . . . she shuddered. Anyway, who was to say he would not still decide to get rid of her after a decent interval?

"I decided that this time I wanted to marry for love," she said resolutely.

There was a silence, while the three men stared back at her. Nicholas Blake consideringly, the viscount with pleased amusement, and Owen with a bleak sort of longing.

"I see," Blake replied at last. "But what about a temporary arrangement? I believe the last thing Sir Theo would want to hear is that you were getting married to another man. And announcing your engagement would, I am certain, sting him into action. We need to flush him out, Your Grace, and I believe that would do the trick."

"He's dangerous." Owen reminded him. "And that would put the duchess in danger."

"A means to an end, dear boy," the viscount said, with an admiring look at Blake.

"We just have to find someone to take on the role of the fiancé," Blake said. "Sir Theo will certainly want to remove him or the duchess from the picture before the wedding could go ahead. He wants her to remain a widow so he can inherit when she dies. Would it be presumptuous of me to offer myself for that role, Your Grace?"

"No!" Owen was on his feet, looking furious. "If she is going to marry anyone then it is me!"

Ellis blinked at him, and then gasped as he fell to his knees in front of her.

"Marry me," he said, his voice dropping to an intimate level. He was gazing into her eyes, his own bright with determination and his curls even more tangled than usual. There was even a smudge of charcoal on his cheek to complete the picture of the overwrought artist.

And oh God, she wanted to say yes, so, so much. "You would

be in danger," she said weakly. "Owen, I couldn't put you in danger. What if something happened to you?"

"I don't care about that," he retorted recklessly. "Say 'yes' Ellis."

Chapter Twenty

OWEN FELT QUITE giddy. He was asking Ellis to marry him so that he could protect her, and if she refused . . . he wasn't sure what he would do. He didn't want to think about it.

Her hands were in his now, and he was still on his knees, and she was looking at him, her beautiful brown eyes glassy with tears. The two other men were watching, probably shocked into silence, but he didn't care. He hadn't liked Blake from the moment he saw him smirking at Ellis, and if Blake was affianced to Ellis, even if it wasn't true, he wasn't sure he could stop himself from punching him in the face.

"Yes."

He blinked. Had she said it?

"Yes, I will pretend to marry you," she added, with a wry twist of her lips. "But if there is even a hint that Theo has his sights set on you, Owen, we must stop this immediately. I will not have you hurt on my account."

He wondered why she thought being hurt on her account mattered to him. He was not going to let Theo have her, that was for certain, and he would do everything in his power to stop it. Afterward . . . well, if she wanted to call the whole thing off that was up to her. Even though Owen knew in his heart he would be perfectly happy to marry her for real.

Except that he was an artist, and she was a duchess with the chance of far better prospects when it came to marriage.

He got to his feet. "That's settled then," he said. "What next?"

Blake looked stunned, and the viscount was beaming.

"We announce it," Blake said, regaining his senses. "The duchess will need to pretend the engagement is genuine. For that reason, we can't have her skulking here. She must go to her sister's town house. Don't worry, I will keep a close watch on her. I have already hired several handy fellows to provide continuous protection."

"And then what do we do?" Owen said, feeling as if he was being left out. "We just wait?"

"Exactly. We wait and catch him in the act."

"Blake knows what he's doing," the viscount interjected.

Blake nodded at the older man. "I will do everything in my power to see this comes to a swift conclusion," he said. "Now, I suggest you prepare a notice for the newspapers. I am aware you are still in mourning, Your Grace, but that can't be helped. Better to be gossiped about than dead."

Owen felt his blood turn icy at the thought of Ellis lifeless, her vibrant beauty still and cold. He might lose her from his life after this was over, but at least she would be alive. It certainly put things in perspective, and he determined not to let Blake rankle him.

"I will escort you to your sister's house," Blake was saying in that "I am in charge, don't cross me" voice. "Tomorrow you will receive callers."

Ellis didn't look overly pleased by this. "You are making a mistake. Sophia won't want—"

"I will prepare the ground," Blake spoke over her. Owen clenched his teeth. "I have already sent a message to the Duchess of Oldney to inform her that you will be arriving almost immediately."

Owen opened his mouth, but Ellis beat him to it. "You take a great deal upon yourself, Mr. Blake."

"All part of the service," said the arrogant fellow. "Now, go and pack, if you please, and I will see that you reach the Oldney house safely."

"I will take her," Owen retorted. "She is *my* fiancée."

"Dear boy," the viscount sighed wearily. "You must let Blake do his job."

Owen was tempted to stand firm, but he knew his uncle was right. He needed to step back for now. There would be enough for him to do in the morning.

Ellis rose to her feet. She looked pale, as well she might. Owen wanted to take her in his arms, but even if that were possible she had a remote look. As if she was only just maintaining her equilibrium.

"I will go and tell Polly to pack again," she said, and left the room.

Blake stayed a moment, looking from Uncle Steven to Owen, before announcing in that smug voice, "I'll make sure everything is in place for the journey," and then he left, too.

Owen and his uncle were alone.

The viscount was giving him a doubtful look. "Are you sure, Owen? I've never known you to be this impetuous before."

"Very sure," he said.

Uncle Steven grimaced. "You do know Blake never had any intention of being the duchess's fiancé? He already knew you would declare yourself."

"But he looked so surprised!"

"He's a very good actor."

Owen wasn't thrilled by the fact that Blake could read him so well.

"This could get very dangerous," the viscount went on. "I wouldn't like to think of you getting hurt. You know I am very fond of you, Owen."

Owen felt his anger seep out of him, and he tried to reassure his uncle. "I won't get hurt. Or at least I'll do my very best not to let that happen. The main thing is that Ellis stays safe. That's all that really matters."

Viscount Hawthorne nodded, looking unusually grave. "Very well then. I can see you're determined to go ahead with it. You always were a stubborn little boy. I will start work on the engagement notices if you want to speak to the duchess before she goes." He gave Owen a knowing glance before moving to pour himself a brandy.

Upstairs, Owen found Ellis in her room, looking tired and flustered. Polly had already repacked the case she had brought with her from the Lodge. She had brought the more respectable gowns Owen had had made for his sitters, but it occurred to him that they were hardly the sort of thing a duchess would wear to go about socially. She must be used to far better.

He looked down at his rather shabby breeches and dull boots. He was not one to care much about how he looked. There was no one to see him at the Lodge. But now he wondered if he should have something more fashionable made up. He didn't want to be a laughingstock or to make Ellis one.

This was turning out to be far more complicated than he had thought when he made his spontaneous proposal.

"Owen?" Ellis had seen him standing there and was frowning at him. "Yes, take that down," she said to Polly, as the maid slipped past them to the door.

"I don't like the thought of you putting yourself in danger," he said. "I wish we'd never left the Lodge. I should have forbidden it."

Ellis's usually warm eyes turned cool. "You have no right to forbid me anything, Owen."

She sounded like a duchess, and he was overstepping.

She went on before he could apologize. "Mr. Blake seems to know what he's doing. We must put our trust in him and hope that this is over soon."

Blake, the know-it-all, Owen thought to himself. "He had better live up to his reputation," he said aloud.

Ellis wasn't listening. "I'm not looking forward to staying

with Sophia," she said dolefully. "We never did get on."

There wasn't much he could say to that, apart from "Stay here," and he knew she couldn't do that. Blake's scheme was in play, and they had to see it through.

"I'll be there first thing in the morning," he said reassuringly.

He could hear Blake downstairs, speaking with his uncle, no doubt waiting for Ellis to appear. Owen would have liked to kiss her and try to regain the closeness they had once had, but he would have to cross the room and wrap his arms around her. And she was watching him with a look that was anything but inviting.

Polly cleared her throat from outside the bedchamber.

"I'm sorry you have to pretend to be engaged to me," Ellis said quickly. "It isn't what I would have wanted for you, Owen."

She seemed very composed for a woman who was in such great peril. But then she had been in danger at the Lodge, too, and she had kept it from him. Owen wondered if he really knew her at all.

There must be something he could say . . .

But there was his uncle, calling up for Ellis to come quickly.

She gave him a brief, brave smile, and then she was gone.

Chapter Twenty-One

At first Ellis thought Sophia looked exactly the same as she had the last time they had been together. Was it really four years ago? So long! Days at Breamore had drifted by, and she had had no desire to return to London, but then neither had Archie. She hadn't greatly missed her sisters, or even her mother, and when they had exchanged letters there had never been a great deal to say. Their lives had taken different paths, and Ellis had been content to allow the gap to widen.

It had been late when Ellis and Blake arrived in the Oldney house in Berkley Square. Ellis had been surprised to find it well lit, as if they had interrupted a party, but when they were shown into a sitting room and Sophia joined them, she was in a robe that covered her nightgown, and her glossy dark hair was in a braid that reached her waist.

Sophia's gaze slid from Ellis to Blake, and she did not seem at all discomposed by her state of undress. In fact, it was as if a bomb had gone off in the room. A frozen sort of bomb.

"Mr. Blake," she said in a chilly voice. "I did not expect to see you in this house."

Nicholas Blake smiled and bowed so low it was an insult. "And I did not expect to be here, Your Grace."

"What is this about my sister being in danger? Just as well my husband is away. You would already be out of the door."

They knew each other, Ellis realized. She also understood they disliked each other intensely.

"Your sister is in need of your protection," Blake said quietly, as if he was remonstrating with a child. "I would have thought you would be keen to assist."

Sophia glared at him a moment more. "You can go," she said. "Ellis and I need to talk."

He hesitated, as if he would have liked to stay and say more, but then he bowed and with an apologetic glance at Ellis, left the room.

"*That* man," Sophia hissed. "He is well-named."

"Well-named?" Ellis repeated, confused.

"Blake. *Snake.*" Sophia waved a hand as if to dismiss him and focused on her sister. She had made no move to embrace her, or take her hands, but Ellis told herself that wasn't odd because they weren't close.

"I'm sorry to arrive without warning," Ellis said, and suddenly she felt very tired and rather depressed. "Mr. Blake thought my being here was the best solution. It has been a rather peculiar few weeks. I did not mean to drag you into it. If you point me to my room you can go back to bed."

Sophia ignored her. "Blake said in his message that you were in danger. You can hardly expect me to go back to bed after reading that."

Now that Ellis looked at her more closely she could see the shadows under her sister's eyes and the pinched look to her mouth. "I do not want to worry you," she said carefully. "There is no need to be worried. When we heard mother was away . . ."

"Mother is in the north of the country with Catherine. Catherine is to be married again. If you visited us occasionally you would have known that before now."

"Married?" She *was* surprised. Catherine's elderly husband had made her so unhappy that she had doubted her elder sister would ever marry again.

"Yes. To a man who loves her deeply," Sophia added, as if reading her mind. "Catherine deserves to be happy this time."

"I am glad to hear it."

Ellis still felt as if there was something she was missing. Sophia was a beautiful woman, but she had never been easy to read. There was a hardness about her, a brittle shell around her, and as far as Ellis could remember it had never cracked to show the feelings beneath. Now that shell looked a little worn.

"Why did you never come to see me and Mother, not even when Catherine visited recently?"

"I . . . I was busy," Ellis stumbled on the words, knowing them to be a lie.

"Not that busy," Sophia scoffed. "Do you know what I think, Ellis? I think you are selfish."

It was a shocking thing to say. Ellis's eyes widened in hurt. She *was* hurt, so she hit back.

"Selfish! Because I do not visit people who have no interest in me? Who have never been interested in me? I was glad to get away from you all, so why would I visit, even for a day?"

Sophia's mouth tightened and the pinch between her brows scored her perfect skin. "Of course, we care about you! *I* care about you! What makes you think I do not?"

Ellis was closer to her now, although she could not remember taking the steps to bring her there. "When I was a child, you tried to lose me in the woods. I wanted to play with you and Catherine, but you laughed and said I couldn't. You didn't want me with you. I was a nuisance, you said. Later, when I was forced to take my place in society, you either ignored me or told me to stay away from you, because I was an embarrassment. You have never cared about me, so why should I care about you?"

Sophia's eyes shimmered with tears. It was so unexpected, Ellis found her own eyes stinging.

"We were children," Sophia said at last. "Children can be cruel. I did not mean it, any of it, and if you thought I did, then I am sorry. As for ignoring you when you made your debut . . ."

She took a shaky breath. "The crowd my husband runs with . . . you should be grateful I kept you away from them, Ellis. I was trying to ensure your safety!"

Ellis knew when Sophia was lying, and she wasn't lying now. Had she really been protecting her younger sister? Confused, Ellis wondered if she had allowed childhood resentments to influence her thinking. She found she didn't know what to believe.

Sophia sat down in a chintz covered chair. "You'd better tell me why you're here before my husband returns from whatever cesspit he is currently inhabiting."

That deserved some comment, too, but Ellis wasn't sure what to say. She had always disliked the Duke of Oldney, but now it seemed her sister disliked him, too. Almost as much as she disliked Nicholas Blake.

Sitting opposite Sophia, Ellis started her story at the beginning, because it was suddenly important to share everything. Her marriage to Archie, his death, Theo's plotting. When she reached the point where Owen proposed marriage to her, Sophia snorted with amused exasperation.

"Oh Lord," she said. "He's beyond smitten."

"He is chivalrous, that is all."

"If you say so."

Ellis ignored her and finally reached the point in the story where they were now.

By then it was very late, and Ellis's eyelids were drooping. Sophia had propped her chin on her hand and was gazing into space, as if she were revisiting the story in her head.

"This engagement is simply a ruse to trick Sir Theo into acting hastily? And it was something Blake came up with?" she said at last.

"Yes." She shot a glance at Sophia. "I am in love with him."

"Blake?" her sister's voice was a screech.

"No, of course not. With Owen, Lord Lyndhurst. He doesn't know that. He is an honorable gentleman, and when I think he is being forced into something dangerous, that he may be *hurt* . . ."

Sophia rolled her eyes. "I'm sure he's very happy to be 'forced' into marrying a wealthy duchess, Ellis. You are naïve. You always were, which was why I did not want you running with my set when you first came out in society. They would have eaten you alive."

Ellis wanted to tell her there was a difference between distancing her sister to protect her and leaving her to stumble her way miserably through an unfamiliar landscape. But what was the point? She was here now, and Sophia seemed willing to take her in. To pick a fight would be petty.

"I've had your bedchamber prepared," Sophia said, watching her face and probably reading it quite well. "You should go up and get some sleep. Blake has men outside on watch. He has a reputation to uphold, so you are perfectly safe."

"Thank you." Ellis rose to her feet.

"I will see you in the morning," Sophia continued. "I expect your ardent suitor will be calling at an unfashionably early hour."

Ellis felt herself warm at the thought of Owen, but she was also worried. He had not seemed happy when she left him earlier, and she wasn't sure if it was because she had dragged him into this mess, or because he had changed his mind about wanting to pretend to be engaged to her.

She slipped into bed and lay in the darkness, staring at the canopy above. When Owen had knelt before her, demanding she marry him, his eyes fierce and bright . . . her heart had been fit to burst. She had wanted more than anything for that moment to be real.

What would happen when this was over? Would they go their separate ways, him to the Lodge and she to Breamore? The two places were not that far apart, but if Owen didn't want anything more to do with her, then they might as well be on opposite sides of the world.

She would hear news of him through others, whispers of his latest model, or perhaps a woman he was courting. And she . . . she would have to pretend not to care.

Chapter Twenty-Two

WHEN OWEN ARRIVED the next morning, he was met by a supercilious looking butler—London seemed to be crawling with them!—who informed him sourly that Ellis had breakfasted and would be downstairs soon. Then he was led into a room with portraits on the walls and left to kick his heels.

He spent his time examining the painted faces. They were a grim lot, and the lack of resemblance to the Mallory sisters led him to assume these were the Duke of Oldney's ancestors. One of them, a plump gentleman on a horse with a sword in his hand, seemed to be riding into battle, but Owen doubted the enemy would be capable of anything but laughter.

Once upon a time he had hoped to be a portrait painter, but he had become so successful with his risqué pictures it would feel like going backward if he were suddenly to begin painting faces. Or would it? Perhaps this feeling of malaise he had experienced over the past year, before Ellis reinspired him, meant he was due a change.

He considered the man on the horse, and decided how differently he would have approached such a subject. He even felt a growing prickle of excitement at the idea.

"Owen."

He spun around, all thought of the plump horseman forgotten. Ellis stood framed in the doorway, smiling at him, her cheeks flushed and her dark eyes warm. Relieved the cool woman from last night was gone, he moved toward her.

"Ah, Lord Lyndhurst, I presume." Sophia's droll tones accompanied her into the room. She had a queenly air to her, and Owen remembered Ellis saying her sister was at the center of the most fashionable society clique.

"Your Grace," he bowed.

Sophia swept past him. "I believe the engagement notice will be in the newspapers this morning. Mr. Blake is nothing if not efficient."

"My uncle is acquainted with the owners of *The Times*," Owen said.

Ellis had an anxious look. "If Theo is still at Breamore, he will not know for some days yet."

"He's not at Breamore. Oldney saw him last night in one of his clubs," Sophia said, and she grimaced when they turned to her. "They are acquaintances. 'Friends' when it suits them."

Owen wasn't sure what to say about that, and he could see Ellis was also taken aback. "They are *friends*? But he is vile!"

Sophia shrugged but she looked uncomfortable. "I spoke to Oldney and told him he is not to associate with Sir Theo again."

Was she expecting to be obeyed without question? Owen doubted it. He could not imagine the Duke of Oldney being the sort of man who listened to his wife.

But Sophia had moved on. "I suppose we must take a drive in the park this morning. It will kill two birds with one stone. People will see that Ellis has not mysteriously disappeared and is in fact very much alive, and at the same time we can introduce them to your fiancé."

Ellis exchanged a glance with Owen, and he knew neither of them was looking forward to making a show of themselves in front of strangers. Suddenly Hawthorne Lodge seemed a long way away, and he wished he were back there. But he would not abandon Ellis. At least they had their dislike of the social scene in common.

Sophia's carriage was ostentatious and in the latest style, and her friends were numerous. Ellis sat beside Owen, with her hand in his, and every now and again he would give it a comforting squeeze. She was pale with shadows under her eyes, and he suspected he was not much different.

Neither of them had slept.

If he could have held her in his arms . . . but that was no longer possible. Last night he had ached for her, and not just in a physical sense. He had sat up by candlelight and drawn Ellis from memory, sketch after sketch, a feverish exercise that only made him feel worse.

He didn't want a copy of her, a woman on paper. He wanted the real flesh and blood woman.

Owen glanced at her profile under her pretty straw bonnet, which was decorated with so many ribbons and flowers it looked like a small garden. Now that he looked closely, he could see she was dressed in the sort of finery that could only have come from a top London modiste. Her sister must have lent her the clothing because there had been nothing like this in the wardrobe at the Lodge to make her look so elegant and worldly. Was it wrong of him to wish her back in the turquoise satin?

Their days in his study, she sprawled on the velvet chaise longue, he on his chair . . . he missed them. He wanted them back again.

An awareness of eyes upon him brought him out of his thoughts, and he glanced up to find Sophia watching him. Was she deciding whether she could trust him and whether he was good enough for her sister? Owen suspected he was failing on both counts.

"Smile, Lord Lyndhurst," she said quietly, smiling herself. "You are not going to your execution."

The greetings and conversations carried on, and it was only when he noticed how Ellis looked even paler and her lips were trembling with exhaustion that Owen decided enough was enough. He leaned forward and said in an undertone to Sophia, "I think your sister needs some peace and quiet. Let us return to the house, Your Grace."

Sophia raised her eyebrows as if she was going to argue, and then she looked at Ellis. She stilled, and her eyes narrowed. Owen was prepared to insist, but he was relieved when a moment later Sophia instructed their driver to turn for home.

With Ellis resting in her room, and Sophia obviously busy with domestic matters, Owen returned to his uncle's house, where he found the viscount ensconced with Nicholas Blake in the library.

They looked up as Owen entered the room. "You look rather done in, dear boy," his uncle said with a frown. "Has the Duchess of Oldney had you sweeping floors?"

Blake sniggered and Owen glared at him. "We went for a drive in the park, and informed everyone who was anyone that we are engaged. Also, Sir Theo Abergele is in London."

He had barely finished when Blake cut in. "I know. I was just telling the viscount."

Owen sank into one of the comfortable armchairs, breathing in the comforting smells of leather and books and cigars. "And did you know that he is a friend of Oldney?"

This time Blake looked as if he'd swallowed a lemon. "I did know. They deserve each other," he added savagely.

Well, there was some ill feeling there! Certainly, there was a story to be told, but Owen wasn't interested in listening to it.

"Then he will know about the engagement along with every-one else. Do you think he will act soon?" mused Uncle Steven.

"Yes," said Blake. "We know he can't wait until you are married. And how does he know how long the engagement will last? What if they make the decision to elope?" He smirked, as if the idea appealed to him. "Yes, I believe he will make his move as soon as possible and remove the problem before matters get more complicated."

"'The problem' being Ellis," Owen said angrily, glaring.

"Dear boy," his uncle sighed. "No one is insulting your lady love."

"My apologies if it seemed as if I was," Blake said. "I am merely trying to look upon the situation in a pragmatic manner, without emotion."

Owen said nothing, but he was thinking that to do such a thing, for him at least, was impossible. Every time he looked at Ellis, thought about Ellis, he overflowed with emotion. Indeed, behind his quiet exterior, he was a passionate man. Perhaps that was why he needed his art, to channel those feelings into something productive.

Once Blake left, Owen decided he would visit Hugh Madrigal. He had the drawings he had completed for the new series, and he knew Hugh would be excited to see them.

It was only when they had greeted each other, and he was watching Hugh rifle through the drawings, that Owen began to have doubts. When Hugh held up the one of Ellis looking well-kissed and gave a low whistle, he was glad he had not brought the more explicit drawings, because the thought of his friend gawping at them made him feel quite ill.

"Owen, this is the best work you have ever done, and I have said that quite a few times. Remarkable. You always exceed my expectations." Hugh took another look through them as Owen sat opposite him in the publisher's office, trying not to shuffle with discomfort. "Is the series finished?" Hugh looked up. "I want it finished as soon as possible."

"I *will* finish it," he said, but even as he spoke Owen wondered if that was true. "Something has come up that I have to deal with here in London."

Hugh gave a dramatic sigh. He was a dramatic sort of person. "You know this book will fly off the press, don't you? Who is this lovely vision?" He pointed at the sketch.

Owen tried not to grind his teeth. The thought of other men salivating over Ellis's image, and Hugh was as close to salivating as he got, gave him a squirmy sensation in his stomach. He did not want all those eyes on Ellis. He did not want them imagining themselves to be the mysterious lover that she was trying to seduce. It was *Owen* she was imagining as she undressed and displayed herself. It was only ever going to be him.

"She may object to the use of her face," he said carefully. "I may have to rearrange her features to make her less recognizable."

Hugh frowned. "Oh. That would be a great pity. I think her face is what will sell these, Owen. You need to keep her face."

Owen suspected that was true, but he didn't want to agree to it.

"Can't you persuade her to allow us to print them as they are?"

Owen mumbled something, which Hugh seemed to take as a yes. "Finish them and then we can talk about the publishing date. I can just imagine your patrons' faces. I think we will have a hit on our hands."

Owen smiled, pretending an elation he was not feeling.

As he left Madrigal's offices and set off down the street, he pondered the awkward situation.

He had never truly wanted to go to an art academy run by stuffy old men. He wanted to be free to express himself as he wished, but he also wanted others to appreciate his work. Hugh certainly appreciated it, and his growing clientele suggested he wasn't alone. But now he found himself reconsidering his choice of profession. The thought of Ellis's face being in front of so many others, along with her risqué poses . . .

He didn't need the money he was making. He wasn't a spendthrift and he lived quietly in the country, and apart from that he was his uncle's heir. Did that mean he could change course if he wanted to?

His choices were simple, it was either change course or allow his intimate moments with Ellis to be shown to the world. What should he do?

The answer came to him, clear and resolute.

Chapter Twenty-Three

ELLIS STARTED IN surprise when Owen was announced. She had been sitting, staring into space, feeling particularly low. She hadn't been at all sure why she was feeling like this, apart from the obvious mess with Theo, but now Owen was here, and everything seemed to brighten.

It was as if the sun had come out.

He looked pleased to see her but there was an uncertainty about his smile as he took her hands in his. He surveyed her with his bright, focused gaze.

"You look better," he announced.

"I am." She squeezed his fingers. "Thank you for reminding Sophia that we are not all as indefatigable as she."

"It was rather an ordeal, wasn't it? Will there be many more like that, do you think?"

Ellis grimaced. "Unfortunately, she has a list of events we must attend. I think she is enjoying herself."

It was true, her sister had thrown herself wholeheartedly into the engagement, in a way Ellis had never seen before. As if she were actually invested in her sister's happiness, or at least in keeping her alive until Theo could be captured. Perhaps Sophia was bored? She was certainly unhappy.

Owen nodded but he didn't appear to be listening. "Ellis," he said suddenly, breaking into her meandering conversation about a ball to be held that evening. "I have something I need to tell you."

She stopped. She felt as if icicles were forming in her heart. He was going to tell her he no longer wanted this fake engagement. He was going to tell her he could not be with her anymore. He was going—

"I am not going to allow Hugh Madrigal to publish the drawings of you."

They stared at each other. He seemed to be holding his breath, waiting, and she was trying to rearrange her thoughts from the ones she had imagined.

"You're not . . . but I thought this was a new series and it was important, and Madrigal was keen to—"

"He was. He is. He thinks it will be a hit." Owen looked down at their entwined fingers. "I just couldn't. The thought of you being ogled by all those men."

"And women," she reminded him.

He ignored that. "I can't do it. It would make me insane with . . . with . . ."

"Jealousy?" she whispered.

He nodded jerkily. His gaze on hers was earnest and worried. "Does that make me a selfish person? Are you angry with me? You seemed to be looking forward to your pictures being out in the world."

She couldn't find an answer. His hair was untidy, as if he had been tugging at his curls as he imagined the world looking at her in those wonderful drawings of his. Was he truly willing to forgo what she knew he expected to be a much sought after picture book? Was he prepared to set aside his own personal triumph because he was . . .

Ellis leaned forward. "Owen, are you in love with me?"

Her heart was beating hard as she awaited his answer.

He was gazing into her eyes, as if willing her to believe him. "Yes, *cariad*," he whispered. "God, yes!"

And then they were kissing, wildly, passionately, as if desperate for that connection.

As if neither of them was whole without it.

"I love you, too." She pressed her face against his throat, her kisses landing haphazardly along his jaw line, where the prickle of his beard made her lips tingle. "It seems too soon and yet I know I do. Are we insane, Owen?"

"*I* definitely am," he muttered, and lifted her into his arms, before seating himself on a sofa with her on his lap.

She found his lips again, her tongue tangling with his, and heat rose up inside her, and with it the ache that could only be satisfied by him. He cupped her breast through the bodice of her gown, and she felt her nipple harden, nudging into his palm. She whimpered.

"Last night I thought about climbing up the wall and into your bedchamber," he said, busily unbuttoning her gown.

She managed a shaky laugh. "I'm not sure Mr. Blake's men would know what to make of that."

"That was the only reason I didn't," he said, and then he groaned at the sight of her naked breasts, filling his hands. "I want you, Ellis. I want you every moment of every day, and I don't even mean your body, wonderful though that is. I just want *you.*"

She understood exactly what he meant because she felt the same.

His mouth was on her, licking and sucking, and she lay back against the cushions on the sofa, her hands in his tangled curls. This was bliss, and she had missed it so much. Could she reach her climax from this alone, without his fingers or his mouth or his cock between her thighs?

She thought so, but there was no chance to test the theory because he was rucking up her skirts, warm breath on her skin, and then his tongue slid into her damp heat to find that hard little button.

Ellis bit her wrist to stop herself crying out. It occurred to her that this was a very risky act on their part. Although the door was shut, anyone could enter the room at any moment. Why didn't she care? Because *this* was more important.

Owen was above her now, kneeling between her thighs, and she reached to fumble with the flap of his breeches. But he was ahead of her. His shaft freed, he lay down on top of her and set it at her entrance, and then he pushed inside.

There was a sound outside the door.

They both froze, gazing into each other's eyes, as the sound faded away into silence again. They needed to hurry.

Ellis felt her body around him, swollen and aching and wanting. She pushed herself fully onto his cock and he closed his eyes and looked as if he had gone to heaven. A moment later he was rocking against her, their bodies already so attuned, and she felt herself soaring.

Did she cry out? She may have. Anyway, he was kissing her again, muffling the sounds of ecstasy. He thrust deep inside her, holding himself there, his body trembling, his throat taut as he arched his head back.

And then they lay, replete, in each other's arms.

Ellis was certain that even had Sophia and Oldney and the whole household walked into the room, they would not have been able to move.

Gradually she came back to herself, a little amazed at their daring, and Owen moved to right himself and smooth down her skirts, refastening her bodice.

He smiled at her. "There," he assured her. "As good as new."

"Better than new," she replied.

"Are you angry with me? About the drawings?" he said earnestly, returning to their earlier conversation.

She shook her head, and realizing her hair was almost as wild as his, pushed it back over her shoulders. "No. And I don't want you drawing other women. Does that make me a horrible person, Owen? It is your work!"

Owen smoothed her cheek with his knuckles, lingering. "I'm beginning to rethink my artistic career," he admitted.

"Please . . . you do not need to change yourself for me."

He gave her one of his intent looks. "It isn't that, *cariad*. I will always be someone who expresses himself through his drawings, his paintings, but loving you has made me realize I need more than a hit picture book. You have inspired me, Ellis."

She wanted to ask him to explain, but he was rising to his feet, giving his clothing a last smooth over and a tug, setting himself to rights.

"You said something about a ball," he began. "Sorry, but my thoughts were otherwise engaged."

She smiled up at him through her lashes. "I'm not complaining." Then, with a sigh, she tried to be serious. "Yes, there is a ball tonight. We are to attend."

"I will be there."

"I wish . . ." She shook her head, then admitted, "I miss Hawthorne Lodge, Owen. I was happy there."

"You will be again." His hazel eyes were very green. "I promise, Ellis."

As she watched him leave, Ellis wanted to believe it was true.

Chapter Twenty-Four

T HE BALL WAS everything Owen disliked about society. People. People everywhere. He was introduced to so many of them he gave up trying to remember their names and contented himself with foolishly smiling and giving Ellis besotted looks. Let them see how much he loved her, he didn't care.

He was *in love*.

Sophia was in her element, sparkling like a diamond under the chandeliers, while Viscount Hawthorne chuckled and made up stories about the way in which his nephew and Ellis had first met. Owen wondered if he would be able to remember them next time he was asked, and then told himself it didn't matter. This was all show, all pretence, and once Sir Theo was captured they could go home to their real lives.

All the same, the thought of that "vile" man, as Ellis called him, made Owen anxious. Blake had said he had guards watching them, but Owen could not see them. Was that because they were very good at their jobs? He hoped so, because if they weren't, then it would be up to him alone to protect Ellis. And although he knew he would give his life for her, he wasn't at all sure it would be enough.

Owen was no marksman, and he was no soldier marching bravely into battle. He was an artist who drew pictures. No wonder he was feeling uneasy about his ability to save the life of the woman he loved.

"You have that look again, Lord Lyndhurst," Sophia's voice sounded in his ear, and he jumped. "I promise you are not getting your head chopped off tonight. Although I'm sure some people here would find it excellent entertainment."

"That does not say much for your friends," he said. He gave a surreptitious glance about him, to see if anyone had noticed his downcast expression. There was his uncle telling yet another version of their story, while Ellis was at his side, trying to smile. No, no one was looking at Owen.

"Are any of them my friends?" Sophia seemed to be asking a rhetorical question and changed the subject before he could think of a reply. Her dark eyes, so familiar and yet so different from the ones he knew, were fixed on his. "I was skeptical when my sister told me about you. I believed you to be a fortune hunter."

Was she really going to give him a lecture here, in the middle of a ball? "I am my uncle's heir," he reminded her stiffly. "I do not need a fortune. I have everything I want."

She cocked her head, as if she had discovered a new species of animal. "I believe you actually mean that. And you love Ellis, don't you?"

He felt his cheeks flush and rubbed at his chin to disguise the sensation of being stripped bare. "Yes," he said. "I love her with all my being."

Sophia watched him a moment more and then sighed. "You make me feel quite jealous," she said. "I don't know why. Because the thought of living in the country with not a party for miles would be the worst thing I could imagine."

Owen grinned. "And yet it is perfect for me. And Ellis, too."

"Yes, it is."

Owen repeated the conversation to Ellis early the next morning when the interminable ball was finally finished. They were climbing into Oldney's coach. Sophia had gone ahead with a friend, and although Owen suspected this was Blake's doing, he wasn't complaining when it came to spending time alone with Ellis.

The ball had been held at a country house in Hampstead and now they had to cross the heath to return home. Until now he had thought nothing much of it. But as they rumbled into the darkness, only the moon and the coach lanterns to show them the way, he realized what a perfect place this was for an ambush.

Ellis smiled at the thought of her sister being jealous of herself and Owen.

"She is unhappy," she said. "At least Archie was a lovely man, even if he would have preferred to marry Elijah. Sophia is stuck with Oldney, and he is horrible."

"I am yet to meet him," Owen admitted. "Why wasn't he there tonight?"

"He was. He was in the card room the whole time. He has no interest in dancing. At least he has no interest in dancing with his wife."

Owen reached for her hand. Her glove was a barrier between their bare skin, and he began to peel the silk from her, so that he could kiss her fingertips, one by one.

"I do love you," she said, her voice low and particularly husky. "Do you think we could ask the coachman to stop for a little while, so that we can sneak off into the trees?"

"When we are married, we won't have to sneak off," he said, and then stopped. Suddenly he felt as if his euphoria had popped like a bubble. "That is . . . will you still want to marry me when this is over?"

She laughed. "I've wanted to marry you since I first saw you," she declared.

Just as a gunshot broke through their cozy moment. Another followed, loud and frightening, and so close he was sure he could smell the gunpowder.

Ellis cried out, and a man appeared at the coach window. Owen saw the shape of him, his face covered with a kerchief, and the raised pistol. He didn't remember moving, but he must have, because suddenly he was lying across Ellis and she was screaming, and then there was a flash.

Being shot hurt. He had always imagined it would, just not this much. He lay, stunned, feeling the warm blood soaking into his jacket, and the world around him becoming strangely blurry. Like a nicely rendered chiaroscuro. Ellis was calling his name, her hands pressing on him as she tried to staunch the bleeding.

He groaned. There was movement outside the coach and then shouting. He supposed that was Blake's men tackling the culprit. For a moment he wondered if this was just an ordinary, everyday highwayman, and how that might upset Blake's carefully laid plans, and he heard himself chuckle.

Ellis cried out. "Owen? Owen! Oh, help, he's been shot! He's delirious."

The coach had stopped now, and the door was flung open. Owen felt himself turned over and settled back on his seat. He was in a great deal of pain, but he asked if Ellis was unharmed, because that was more important.

"Yes, yes, you saved her life," Blake said impatiently, but Owen could hear the worry in his voice. "Ah," he added, after a moment of prodding and poking, "it went into your shoulder and out the other side. I don't think anything is broken, but the surgeon will see to you. He is somewhere about."

Blake, it seemed, had planned for every eventuality.

"Let me go!" The voice came from close by, and Ellis cried out in fear.

Owen tried to rally, gritting his teeth against the pain. "Is that him? Sir Theo?"

Blake's teeth flashed white. "Yes, we have him. Everything went exactly to plan."

Owen wanted to point out that him being shot wasn't part of the plan, but Sir Theo's voice came again.

"Let me go! I have done nothing wrong. Archie didn't even deserve to be duke. His marriage was a sham—lies, all lies! I am the rightful heir. *I* am the rightful—"

His desperate shouts stopped then quite suddenly, and Blake breathed a sigh of relief. "Lock him up," he ordered his men, before turning back to Owen. "Your lady love is safe, and you are a hero, Lord Lyndhurst. How does it feel? You will have invitations to every entertainment on offer for the remainder of the Season."

Owen groaned. What did it say about him that the idea of gadding about caused him more anguish than his wound?

Blake was gone, his presence replaced by the surgeon, who preceded to examine him. Owen tried to be stoically silent, but it hurt a great deal and by the end he felt rather faint. At least the bullet had not broken any bones or hit anything life ending, and once it was cleaned and bandaged, he would feel more the thing.

The coach began to move again, slowly, for which he was grateful.

"My poor, brave love." He felt a gentle hand smoothing back his hair, and a soft kiss on his brow. "Never mind, we can go home as soon as you are well enough."

Owen smiled. Then opened his eyes. "What of the marriage ceremony?"

Ellis was close to him, and he could see the dried streaks of tears on her cheeks. "I think Sophia wants us to marry here," she said. "I feel I should agree. She has been good to us, and I have a lot to make up for."

Owen didn't ask what that meant, he was happy just to allow Ellis to stroke him and kiss him. Sir Theo was dealt with, and Ellis was safe. Anything else could wait.

Epilogue

One year later

"LIKE THAT."

Owen stepped back and surveyed Ellis's pose. She was reclining on the chaise longue, dressed in the turquoise satin, her hair loose about her. He smiled. She was beautiful. She was also looking well-kissed because she was.

"Sophia sent me a letter," she said, trying not to move her mouth, which made him smile again.

"And what did she say?" The Duke of Oldney had died not long after Sir Theo was arrested, and in somewhat mysterious circumstances.

"Not a great deal. Now her period of mourning is over for Oldney, she is returning to society again and very glad of it. Although she is planning to visit Catherine and her husband and son and the new little one. Reading between the lines, I thought Sophia was sounding a little melancholy."

Owen had made the preliminary sketches for the portrait, and now he was ready to begin laying on the paint. It was exciting, and he already felt as if this was going to be his masterpiece.

Several local dignitaries had asked to sit for him, as well as some aristocrats. Since the incident with the coach and Sir

Theo—and his daring deed—he had become rather a celebrity, and people wanted to be painted by him. Hugh Madrigal had been most unhappy when Owen told him there would be no more salacious drawings, but his previous works were still selling well, so he really didn't have much to complain about.

"Ellis?" The voice was tentative, and a handsome young man with fair hair peeped around the door. "Ah, there you are. I should have known."

"Elijah, you are interrupting," Owen told him with a frown he didn't really mean. Elijah was someone you could never be cross with for long. He lived on the grounds of Breamore now with Rowan the groom. Their time in the mountains seemed to have brought to the fore feelings they didn't know they could have for each other. They were, so Ellis said, rapturously happy.

Breamore was a beautiful place. Owen and Ellis resided here most of the time, although they often retreated to Hawthorne Lodge—like Marie Antoinette, playing at being commoners. Owen didn't mind where he was, as long as Ellis was with him.

"Oh, very nice." Elijah had come to gawk at the half-finished work. "Saucy, too. Joan was sure it would be."

Ellis sat up, breaking the pose. "What do you mean, *saucy?*"

Elijah chuckled and winked and left the room. No doubt Joan and Polly would be waiting to have a laugh with him. The two women were at Breamore too, and Joan revelled in her new role as housekeeper at such a grand establishment. Their old housekeeper had retired after Theo's arrest, informing them she needed a quieter life.

"He was teasing," Owen said and, setting down his brush, came to sit beside her.

Ellis smiled. "I'm glad to see him in such high spirits again." She hesitated. "Sophia wants us to come with her. To see Catherine."

Owen leaned in to kiss her cheek, lingering. "Then let's. I've been thinking. You may not agree but . . . I wondered if I could do a portrait of the three of you. The three Mallory sisters. Not as you were when you took the *ton* by storm, but as you are now. Older, happier, and even more beautiful."

Ellis's eyes had widened. "Oh, that sounds . . . I would love it! And I think Catherine and Sophia would love it too. In fact, I'm sure they would."

LATER, AS ELLIS got ready for bed, she thought of the portrait and smiled to herself. The three of them as they were now, rather than the naïve girls they had once been. Mrs. Mallory might wrinkle her nose at it, but what did that matter? Besides, her mother was no longer the ambitious woman she had been—these days she seemed perfectly content to mind Catherine's children.

Owen was lying on his back on their bed, watching her, and she pretended not to notice as she began to undress, taking her time about it. Her stockings, rolled down slowly, slowly, and then her gown eased from her shoulders, puddling at her feet. A little wriggle to remove her chemise.

Owen groaned at the sight of her naked body. "I'm dying here," he said.

Ellis ignored him, taking the pins from her hair one by one. She was still doing that when suddenly he appeared behind her, as naked as she, and lifted her up into his arms. She shrieked as he carried her back to their bed.

He was already kissing her before he lay her down, and Ellis wrapped her arms and her legs around his long, lean body, and told herself she was the luckiest woman in the world. Their kisses grew deeper and hotter and more passionate, and Owen lifted her hips and put his mouth onto her.

She tried to speak but the words were all muddled, and his shoulders shook with laughter. Although he didn't stop what he was doing. Not until she cried out in glorious pleasure. When she returned to herself, he was propped up on top of her, watching her and smiling.

She reached up to stroke the curls out of his eyes. "We are so lucky to have found each other, Owen. When I set out in the coach to escape Theo, I never imagined I would find such sanctuary as I did in Hawthorne Lodge, with you."

"As much as I loathe Sir Theo, he did do one good thing. He sent you to me. If he had not been so vile, we might have spent our whole lives never knowing each other."

"Somehow I think we would have met," she said dreamily. "We were destined to be together—I know it. Perhaps I would have asked you to Breamore to paint my portrait."

"Portrait painting is a very slow process," he teased. "I probably would have stayed forever."

"'Forever' sounds perfect."

He took her in his arms and held her close to his heart, and Ellis smiled. *This* was happiness. This was everything she had ever wanted, and more.

About the Author

Sara Bennett is an Australian bestselling author of Historical Romance. She has written many books set in various time periods—Medieval, Regency and Victorian—as well as Paranormal Romance under the name Sara Mackenzie.

She started her career writing under the penname Deborah Miles for Mills & Boon. Her books have been published by Avon/Harper Collins, and are available worldwide. She has also written numerous Australian Women's Fiction books as Kaye Dobbie. Currently she alternates between publishing independently and with traditional publishers.

Sara has been a finalist for the RITA award (Romance Writers of America) and the RUBY (Romance Writers of Australia).

Sara lives in Victoria, Australia, in an old house in a goldrush town, with her husband and two important cats. She would love to spend more time in the garden but there are just too many stories to be written.